Don't judge Me

Part 1

Lillian Moore

Moorelillian2025@outlook.com

Copyright © 2025

All Rights Reserved

ISBN: 978-1-966468-42-4

Dedication

I would like to dedicate this first series to those who inspired me to write this book. I thank you for the many of phone conversations, the late nights, drinking, getting drunk conversations, and the information shared amongst each other. Especially in a group. What an experience I received hearing some of the stories and actually playing it out in my head as the stories were shared. I appreciate you in every way. I only hope that I brought the story to life as it were shared. I'm not gonna call you out by name, but please note that you made this book possible for me to write. So I thank you.

Acknowledgement

I would like to thank my 9th grade English teacher, Mr. Depheeni of Beeber Middle School for giving out an assignment to write a poem. Without my knowledge, the poem that I wrote was entered into a contest and declared a winner. I received an 'A,' and he received the cash prize. I didn't care too much about the money. However, what I cared about was the fact that someone heard what I had to say, and they enjoyed it. Ever since then, I've been writing. So, shout out to all the teachers who wakes up the skills within their students.

Contents

Dedication v

Acknowledgement vii

About the Author xi

Preface xiii

Introduction 1

Chapter 1: Meeting John 4

Chapter 2: The Bullshit Handbook............................... 10

Chapter 3: The Day After 37

Chapter 4: Let's Get It On 51

Chapter 5: Bitch Ass Nigga.. 62

Chapter 6: Meeting My Husband.................................. 75

Chapter 7: His Situation... 82

Chapter 8: My Young Bull.. 90

Chapter 9: Drunken Love 99

Chapter 10: The Aftermath...121

Chapter 11: Lesson Learned... 130

Chapter 12: The Reunion 136

Chapter 13: Never Letting Go...................................... 147

Chapter 14: A New Thing 159

Chapter 15: Two Men And A Young Bull................... 165

Chapter 16: Temperature Rising..................................191

Chapter 17: The Test 202

Chapter 18: Choices.. 205

Chapter 19: Mind, Body And Soul................................211

About the Author

I am the youngest of three girls with a younger brother. Therefore, I was seen, not heard. I had a lot to say, but I was told that I talk too much, so I said nothing. Therefore, every thought and feelings that I had would build up inside then released in a worst way. My whole entire childhood was based on me not being able to have the type of discussions that I needed to have. Until I wrote my first poem called "When My Father Died." That poem was based on how I felt sitting there at his funeral without any sorrow or care. Writing that poem was really therapeutic for me. It gave me the opportunity to release the guilt of me not caring that he was no longer here on paper. I didn't know why I felt like that, maybe because we never had a connection. However, I couldn't talk about it, so I chose to write about it. And after putting it on paper I felt so relieved that I no longer wanted to talk about my feelings to anyone. I just pulled out a pen and a book and started writing. And that's how it began.

Preface

Stacey is a middle-aged woman who's just coming out of a ten-year relationship with a man who did nothing but bullshit her the whole time. And because of that, she lost herself and all feelings of trying to find mister right. So, she decides while working on her mind, body, and soul, she would just have good, long, and exciting sex with the man that can handle he sex drive. However, because she couldn't find that one person that can match her drive, she becomes promiscuous. Leaving no room to catch feeling, so that there was no room for lies or deceits.

Introduction

This is for the ladies only; I don't care whether you're White, Black, Asian, or whatever ethnic background you are. We as women have to take a stand against these no-good cheating ass men and treat them the way they are supposed to be treated. A motherfucking King will treat his woman like the Queen she is by being a faithful man that will only give himself to her and only her. And it will only be about her.

We have to stop putting these motherfuckers on a pedestal if that's not where they belong. Before you wake up 51 years old, alone and feeling like so many of your good years have been squandered with a man that you hoped to hang up his hat full of lies, cheating, and selfishness, and love you back the way that you love him. With commitment, understanding, loyalty, and all of the above. To sum it all up, RESPECT. Why can't we, as women, do the things that men do? Why must we go out and get toys to make us have orgasms when we're not satisfied sexually? Why can't we have multiple partners like our spouses and still remain with each other? After all, I think we women have a sweet tooth, too. We like to have the icing on the cake, just like the men. However, we are different from men, meaning that we are not equal to. But, fuck it, if you have more than one partner, why can't we. The other women is around for a reason. For the same reason, another man would be around. The saying is, "What you won't do, another dude would."

So, if you come into a relationship with a man and you know that he is not the one for you because you're going through a lot of bullshit in the first three months of getting to know each other. Ladies, that shit is not going to change. The only thing that's going to happen is that the longer you stay with him it's going to get worse. So, stop thinking that your kitty-kat can change a man's fucked up ways. If you get with a man who's well into his 50s, who has been married and divorced, or whose never been married, there is a reason; take it from me. Now, if you get with a man that is in his 50s and he's a widow, you might have a chance. You can tell a lot about a man based on their conversations in reference to women, whether it's his late wife or a past girlfriend, mother, or even a strange woman in the streets. But I'm gonna go with his relationship with his mother mostly. If a man loves his mother and treats her like the honorable woman she is for bringing his fucking ass into this world and taking care of him, then he's worth your time. Maybe he just had the wrong woman in his life. However, I've come to this realization that If a man used the word bitch every time he refers to a woman, and you don't correct him on that, sooner than later, you too would become one that he refers to as his bitch. Why? Because he really doesn't respect any women, runaway. And if you decide to stay, use him for what he's worth, fuck it, good sex, money, or his profession. A man that's in a good position can be helpful to some of your needs. Because that fucked up man is only going to make you fall in love with him. Have you depended on him, then treat you like shit. Or, better yet, become his motherfucking case study without you even knowing it. Some motherfuckers are bold enough to tell you that you're a case study as if you're a fucken lab rat. Funny right? Then tells you he wants to get into your head to find out what makes you tick. Isn't that some shit? If a motherfucker isn't telling you much about him, don't tell him much about you because he will, and let me repeat, he will turn that shit around and use it on you in certain situations. And to make matters worse, after giving this person (regardless of race—ignorance, selfishness, and bad behavior apply to anyone) all of your best years, years that someone else might have cherished, those years ended up becoming the worst because the happiness just wasn't there. And the good man that's been after you, chasing you and showing you that he would and could be that man that you need is now being that good man to someone else while you're getting absolutely nothing but good sex, heartaches, and a fucking headache. This is not a story about man-bashing. It's just simply telling the ladies fuck that; let's flip the script on these motherfucking men and stop accepting their bullshit. Yes, it may seem that I'm mad. And yes, I have every reason to be mad, but I'm not because the signs have been there since we started. However, that's another story.

So, people, I'm about to share with you 2 fucking years of my life as to why I am the way that I am. So, ladies and men, if you are reading this, please.

Don't judge me, Men You Made Me This Way.

Chapter 1: Meeting John

I've been in a relationship with four different men who all must have read from the same bullshit-ass handbook. Based on selling the bullshit.

After my 9-year relationship with a bullshitter, I decided to take a breather and just get back into me. We, as women who has a strong desire to be happily married, tend to lose sight of our rights for us. We tend to lose ourselves trying to keep a no-good man who doesn't want to be kept by no longer thinking or caring about what we really need or want from our spouse or in a relationship. But instead, we exchange it for what he wants and needs, hoping that he would stay.

When I first met this man who I had nicknamed King-Ring-A-Ding., I also found out that he calls himself King-Ding-A-Ling. I asked him why. To which he said that the females that he had dealt with in the past said his dick was big. "Well, that remains to be seen," I remember thinking.

When I met him, I happened to be in a dark place. I didn't know whether I was going to have my freedom in the next three months or not for a crime that I didn't commit. The only thing that was on my mind was to find someone to have good, long, and satisfying sex with. Someone who would be able to match my sex drive.

Oh, and let's not forget, a good conversation, too. Because everybody loves that pillow talk every now and then. I can recall the first time we saw each other while crossing paths. The wave to one another was like "Damn," and the look we gave each other was like "I want to fuck you."

"Don't judge me, my sex drive is high, and he looks like he's a good fuck."

So, for the first two weeks of crossing each other's path, I would say about three times a day for five days a week, there was a friendly wave and a sexual look. Until one day, when the time presented itself when I wasn't rushing off to the restroom to avoid having an accident. I felt the heat of his eyes gazing on my ass.

I seized the opportunity to introduce myself. As I walked towards him, I could see his eyes through the light-shaded lens of his glasses as he looked me up and down, watching my hips move in a sensual way. Wearing my uniform skirt, and 3-inch black ankle boots w/blue knee-high stockings that just reached the calf of my legs, revealing the muscle as it made my legs look strong and beautiful. Now, in 3-D, standing right before him, I took the opportunity to talk to him.

Stacey: (in my perky voice) Good morning, my name is Stacey; what's yours?

John: (with a nerdy voice) Good morning, I'm John.

Stacey: Nice to meet you finally.

John: Yeah, I wanted to say something to you, but you were always rushing to the bathroom.

Stacey: Yeah, that's my thing; I drink a lot of fluids.

John: Yeah, I'm just the opposite; I try not to drink as much so I don't have to go.

Stacey: Well, I need this because when I work out, I sweat a lot.

John: How often do you go to the gym?

Stacey: I try to go every day, but if I can't make it every day, then I'll go at least five times a week.

John: I used to work out all the time myself.

Stacey: And you don't anymore?

John: No, I haven't had the time because of my work hours.

Stacey: The best thing that you could do for yourself is to make the time.

John: You're right, I will. My man keeps asking me when I'm gonna start working out with him again.

Stacey: Listen, we're not getting any younger, the last thing that you want to do is to have to take meds just to make it through the day.

John: You're right.

Stacey: I know I'm right, just look at some of these unhealthy ass people. Oh goodness, nature calls; I'll see yah later.

John: You sure will.

He smiled at me, and I back to him. Then I turned around and power walked to the restroom. Once more, I felt the heat on my ass as I walked away, so I added a little something to my walk. "Yeah, baby, watch this ass."

After that introduction and a very small conversation every day for about a month, there were small conversations revealing a little about ourselves to each other. Until one day, he asked whether I had a man or not. Then he said.

John: Well, you don't have to answer that question. I like talking to you, so it really doesn't matter.

Then he handed me his number and said:

John: Here, take my number; you can call me anytime; just tell your man that we're just friends.

I did take his number and thought to myself, "What he's really saying is that I don't care whether or not you have a man, I still want to hit that big ass of yours."

Stacey: My man! I guess someone like myself is supposed to have one of those, huh?

John: Yes, I would think that you do, in fact, I know that you have one of them.

Stacey: No, Sir. And if I did, I would not be taking your number and calling you a friend.

The expression on his face was like, "Yes, I'm one foot in the door." As the weeks passed, the conversations changed; they went from innocent to very personal to sexual. We talked about past relationships. What we liked and disliked. We even spoke about our childhood (school days) and family. He kept my interest as I did his.

However, we both knew what we really wanted, but we just kept the momentum of a good conversation going. I knew that we would become good friends, "friends with benefits, that is it." And if a relationship happened to come out of it, then, that would be fine with me too.

But right now, just friends until I'm done with seeing the way my freedom was going to play out. And to be honest, all I really want to do is fuck, fuck, fuck.

"Don't judge me; I'm a Highly Sexual Person."

Now if we still happen to be fucking each other after my situation is handled, and I come out on top, and a relationship comes out of it. Then I'm cool with that. It's not like he's a bum-ass-dude. He has a good job making good money.

Chapter 2:
The Bullshit Handbook

Okay, almost two months now, and we're still having long conversations, and the anticipation is rising. So, finally, the opportunity presented itself for a possible hook-up. I was kind of excited because I will finally get a chance to see what he's really working with, whether or not he deserves to keep the name King-Ding-A-Ling or become King-Ring-A-ling.

So now the date is put into motion for that Saturday. However, when Saturday morning came, I did hear from him while I was running errands, but after that, no more.

So, when Monday came, he waved and smiled at me like he did nothing wrong. Me being the person that I am, I just looked at the stupid ass grin he had on his face, trying to understand why he is speaking to me after he stood me up.

As he was walking up towards me, I acted like I had to run to the bathroom. But that didn't do the trick as he followed me, calling out my name.

John: Stacey! Stacey!

Stacey: Why are you speaking to me? I'm not fucking with you no more.

John: Why?

Stacey: You know why, Saturday!

John: Wait, let me explain. I'm so sorry, but my boy asked me if he could use my truck to pick up his clothes from his old crib that he shared with his ex. I told him yeah, then he went to go do other shit. I was so fucking mad at him. You know, after showing your picture to him, I think he was low-key hating. There was jealousy written all over his face.

Stacey: Okay, but you still could have called, texted, or, how about this one, answered the damn phone when I called you?

John: I had a couple of beers while I was waiting for him. I must have fallen asleep. Please forgive me. I'll make it up to you.

Stacey: (the finger went up) Strike one.

I still didn't know how I felt about him because I just came out of a relationship with a liar. So yes, I guess I'm not completely over the hurt. And if this nigga really expected me to believe that bullshit, then he has to be the dumb one.

And to be honest, all I wanted was some casual sex with someone who can give it to me the way that I like it without the bullshit. And when I say without the bullshit, I mean no commitment.

Therefore, there are no lies and no expectations, but he wants to add the bullshit anyway. Now I see why I'm by myself.

So let me take the time to step back a little and talk, just to see where his head is.

And like I said, we have spoken about sex before, but now, I really want to know how much he knows. Like, is he really experienced enough for me? I don't know; that's why he probably stood me up.

Psych nah, the woman that he has at home is why he stood me up. But guess what? I'm gonna fuck him anyway. Because, like I said, there is no commitment.

John: So let me tell you my favorite style.

"Now me, being the person that I am, I feel like I must indulge in the conversation to see where he's going with this."

Stacey: What's that?

John: Missionary.

Stacey: Missionary?

John: Yes.

Stacey: Wait! Did I say it like I know what freaking style that is?

John: You don't know what missionary is? Or no one ever did it like that to you.

Stacey: Probably, but who asks while fucking, what style is this? Or who says (in a deep voice) Now I'm gonna fuck you missionary style. Come on, really. So how does it go?

John: I like to throw those legs up and over my shoulder and go deep.

My whole entire face changed.

Stacey: Damnn

John: Which way do you like it?

Stacey: Any way that I can feel you the most.

John: What!!!

We both started laughing.

Stacey: Nah, well, I'm a bit of a control freak when it comes to sex. I don't want to be your bitch; I'd rather you be mine. I love to ride stallions. I like to have full control over it.

John: Shit! I hear you. Oh! Don't forget to feed me my dessert.

Stacey: Really now! Shit, the kitchen is always open for that.

John: I'm all about the foreplay.

Stacey: Well, I have a vibrator for that. But, my nipples, you can suck on them all day. Shit! With a little teeth and my toy.

"Just thinking about that started to get me excited."

John: Are you a squirter?

Stacey: Yes, if you know what you're doing.

He then looked at his watch and saw that he was running late.

John: We'll finish this conversation later.

Stacey: Call me.

John: What time?

Stacey: Anytime.

So, as the day went on, I just kept thinking to myself. "It's been three months already, and damn, I'm so horny for some dick." I heard tall dudes have a lot to give if you know what I mean.

By the next time we spoke again, I was ready to plan a get-together between him and myself. Especially when the conversation about how they used to call him King-Ding-A-Ling came up again. Of course, I just had to ask why, and in his nerdy voice. He said:

John: Because I was not a disappointment in the bed. Every woman that I have ever been with was completely satisfied.

"Shit! Now I'm really like, damn! Let's have it. I didn't have a good shot in a while, and the toys just weren't cutting it no more." Then he said:

John: You know, since you get off earlier than me, I can shoot over, give you what you need, and then go home.

"What you really mean to say is get your shit off, then go home."

Stacey: What time do you get off?

John: Seven.

Stacey: Okay, cool, that gives me enough time to hit the gym. I'll text you my address.

John: Okay.

Later that day, I received a text thirty minutes into my workout saying:

"What's your address?"

I didn't answer it right away because he just seemed too hungry. So, I decided to make him wait by returning a favor from him, standing me up.

"Don't judge me, Yes I'm Being Petty, He Made Me This Way."

So after I was done with my workout, I decided to text him saying:

"I'm kind of tired; we'll link up tomorrow. Cool?"

He texted back: "No, not cool, I was looking forward to coming over there."

I replied: "You waited this long, you can wait a little longer. The kitty-kat will still be wet and tight."

John: Hum.

Now it's about 9 o'clock pm, and my ex is calling me. I don't know why the hell he's calling me. He's my ex for a reason.

So before I answer this call, let me tell you a little something about Steph.

When I first met him 10 years ago, I was in a good place in my life. (Body, mind, and soul). There wasn't nothing, and I do mean nothing, that I worried about. Shit! I was living my best life.

Therefore, I didn't need someone to come in to make me happy; I needed someone to add to it. That meant no fucking drama because, I tell you, these men today act like bitches.

Bitches are the women who always come with the drama. A lady would look past the small shit and keep it moving because she doesn't have time for the nonsense. A bitch is always in his or her feelings.

Anyhow, when I first met Steph, the both of us were stopped on a two-lane street side-by-side, waiting for the light to change. I had my windows down because it was a beautiful summer morning. I heard a man's deep voice saying:

Steph: Excuse me, excuse me.

I turned my head from left to right, wondering where the hell the voice was coming from and who the hell was saying excuse me. Then I heard it again; this time, it was louder.

Steph: Excuse me, Miss.

I looked over to my right, and all I could see was the door of a dump truck and a person with a blue short-sleeved shirt and a light-skinned arm holding the steering wheel. I called out in response:

Stacey: Yes?

Steph: Can I ask you a question?

Stacey: Sure, what is it?

Steph: Do you have a good mechanic?

Stacey: Yes.

Steph: Do you have a good man?

Stacey: No.

Steph: Here, take my number and call me.

I picked up my phone, thinking he was going to verbally give me his number when a piece of paper came flying in the front passenger window. As he pulled off, I picked up the paper and opened it. It had his name and number written on it. And at that time, all I could do was laugh because that was some crazy shit.

Although his game was original, it was also funny. But what was even more funnier was that I didn't even know how the hell he looked. Fuck, he might be looking like what-the-fuck. Return back to sender, put it back in the womb.

I tell you, curiosity can be the worst thing or the best thing. For me, my curiosity always gets the best of me because, for the past couple of weekends, this truck was always parked on the same corner.

Now I'm wondering if that was the corner he was driving to. So, I circled back around and as I came around, I saw a truck parked on the corner.

I slowed down because there were 4 guys standing outside. So, I picked up my phone and called Steph to see which one of them would answer.

OMG, I was so relieved when he picked up the phone and not the other guys. I'm not gonna go in on them; I'm just going to say: they're not my cup of tea.

Now tell me, how do you spell relieve? And please make sure you spell it in all caps because that's how I felt. When he picked up the call, I couldn't help but grin.

Steph: Hello.

Stacey: Hello.

Steph: Who is this?

Stacey: This is Stacey; you just threw your number in my car, so I thought that I would call you and leave you mine.

Steph: Okay, bet.

Stacey: Lock me in; I'm getting ready to work out now, so I'll talk to you in a minute.

Steph: Workout, okay, cool. But can you send me a pic so that I can put it with your name and number?

Stacey: Okay, in a minute.

When we hung up from each other, I went through my phone to find him one of the best pics taken.

The picture that I sent him changed my look completely. That's what lashes, make-up, and a different color wig will do. He didn't believe it was me.

So, I sent him several pics with different color wigs. And he was taken on by the different looks.

After that, we talked on the phone all the time. Either on his way home or while he was still at work.

We would meet up in the park after work because neither one of us was ready to bring the other home.

One Saturday, he invited me out to KFC for lunch. That's when I found out he was cheap.

Stacey: Call me boujee, but I don't eat that shit.

Steph: What do you eat?

Stacey: Not that; I don't do fast foods. That shit ain't no good for you.

Steph: So, you're a health freak?

Stacey: Yeah, like I didn't get this body eating fried food every day.

Steph: Okay, I guess I'm gonna have to find a place to take you then.

Stacey: I know a couple of places, but I'll let you put in the work of finding somewhere.

After that, he would always make plans to do something on a Saturday; however, when Saturday came, the plans would always change. There goes that bullshit again. They're reading out of the same handbook.

It didn't matter to me, though, because I always had something or somewhere to go and do. After all, he was not my man; he was really just a good conversation.

So now I know that he's cheap and also a liar. I still held conversations with him because of his listening skills. And whenever I needed him, he was there.

That's how our relationship started.

One Sunday, we linked up at a motel in New Jersey. The motel wasn't even five-star shit! It wasn't even three.

And because it was only for a couple of hours. It was all good. When we went into the room, we took our clothes off and got into the shower.

With the hot water pouring down over my body, he grabbed my leg and put it up on the side of the bathtub. Then, he got on his knees and started licking my kitty-kat.

OMG, that shit felt too fucking good. Then he took his hands and opened the lip of my kitty, then stuck his tongue inside of me.

Stacey: Awww

I tell you that shower sex was the bomb. The hot water took it to another level. Then, he got up, turned me around, bent me over, and stuck his dick inside of me.

It felt like I was having sex for the first time. It was painful; I screamed as I held on to the knobs of the faucet as he slammed into my kitty.

Then he picked me up, took me to the bed, and gently laid me down on my stomach. Kissing me on my ass, working his way up to my neck, and then whispering in my ear in a soft, deep voice.

Steph: I want to make love to you; I don't want to fuck you.

He turned me around to my side and put one of my legs over his shoulders, covering the other with his body, pinning me down.

Inserting himself in me gently, I reached my arms over my head, grabbing the pillow, squeezing it as he just kept going in and out of me.

As time went on, he started giving me more and more. I let go of the pillow and started pushing into his chest to stop because it was hurting still.

He put my leg down from his shoulder and grabbed my hands, moving them from him to lying it flat down on the bed.

Then he just laid there still inside of me, passionately kissing me. Once I calmed down, he started stroking me again.

Steph: Damn girl. You feel so fucking good.

I was screaming so loud that when I turned my head towards the window, I thought that I saw someone standing there listening.

I pushed him to stop because I saw the shadow. When I got up to see, they were gone.

I stayed peeping through the blinds; when he came over, he put his foot in between my legs, forcing me to open them.

Steph: Spread your legs.

I spread my legs apart, then he grabbed my ass cheeks, spread it open, then put his dick inside of me. He started going crazy back there.

My face was pressed against the window, and with every stroke, there was a bang against the glass.

Stacey: Oh my God, please stop. It hurts.

Steph: I'm sorry; I don't want to hurt you.

He slowed down and just stroked the kitty gently.

Stacey: No! My face is hitting the window.

He bent his knees as if he were doing squats, still inside of me, resting my ass on him as if he were a chair, carrying me backward towards the bed.

When he sat down on the bed, he grabbed my waist, moving me forward and then backward, forcing himself at the very end of my uterus.

I screamed because it was hurting more than it felt good. Then he worked his hands down to my hips and lifted me up with the head of his dick still inside of me.

He turned me around until I was facing him. He sat up, my legs wrapped around his waist as his arms around mine.

We were now face to face, riding each other slowly. Until we both had an orgasm, we both laid down, and then his phone rang.

When he answered the phone, I could tell that he was talking to a female. A female that he said he didn't have.

The fucking disrespect; I started to say something to him while he was on the phone with her talking about football as if he had just got finished watching the game.

But, fuck it, we're just fucking; he's her problem, not mine.

At that time, I realized everything that I needed my next man to be; he wasn't. He's a liar and a cheater, not to mention cheap.

The only thing that he had going for him for me was that he's a good fuck and a good listener.

After this, I started getting frequent calls from him that I just ignored.

Then, the text messages started coming in back-to-back. I saw them, but I ignored it as well. He still stayed persistent in luring me in.

Because he knew where I lived, I would wake up in the morning to flowers and a card sitting in front of my window. Balloons tied down on my side mirror.

Every other day, it was something different, and it never stopped. So, eventually, I gave in. I thought he and his girl were no more.

He said that he was tired, tired of getting hurt and running around with these different women. And that he's ready to settle down.

Now, because he kept pursuing me in such a way after our sexual actions, I thought that my kitty-kat made him want to be a better person, that it wanted him to be with me. To be mines and only mines. He my King and me his motherfucken Queen.

In a matter of months, we went from fucking partners to boyfriend and girlfriend.

Although, there were still issues with him. I tried to look past that because, now, he's in his own place, and we're spending more time together.

The very first time that we spend together was on Valentine's Day. That wasn't just that day; it was the whole weekend. OMG, that was one of the best weekend's that I've ever had with him. Sexing me and spoiling me. I didn't care that his money wasn't long because, at that time, he was giving me exactly what I needed.

When I would leave work and come to him, he would have my bath waiting for me, with a glass of my favorite wine.

On Saturdays and Sundays, he would make breakfast for me because that was the only day that I ate solid food.

He even went out and brought a smoothie machine to accommodate me during the weekdays. The relationship was going in a way that I didn't regret building.

We were meeting each other families. I'm dropping people from my contacts, and he said he was too.

Until I caught him with a girl naked ass posing with her legs opened, exposing her kitty-kat on his phone. Then, to read his reply saying that they were going to hook up.

This motherfucker! I stayed anyway because he came with the bullshit crying game. I fell for it, and guess what? That shit never stopped.

Ever since then, it has always been something about different girls. In the course of us being together for 9 years.

We have been engaged over 3 times with 3 different rings. Every time that he would fuck up, then propose to me again, the diamond had to be bigger and the ring much better than the last.

But, still, he hadn't learned his lesson. It just came to the point that I didn't care; he could have the other girls if he wanted. I was sick and tired.

Although we had very good sex, it just wasn't enough. No matter how much he claims he love me, he just couldn't leave other women alone. So that's why I left his ass. Now, once again like I said, me being the person that I am, I would entertain the nonsense for a while.

He said he wanted to come over and give me a full body massage.

"Now you already know what that means in his head; I want to make love to you in every way. But nigga, for me, it's not making love to me or me making love to you, it's straight-up fucking. I don't love you anymore. However, you can come over and help me go to sleep by giving me that full body massage, then take that ass home."

Damn, like I was only on the phone with him for three minutes, and within the next five minutes, he was knocking at my front door. When I let him in, he had this dumb-ass, Kool-Aid smile on his face. I knew that he had just come from a female's house because he reeked of a female's perfume. And since he didn't get none, he thought these legs were gonna open for his dirty dick ass. Yeah, right nigga, dream the fuck on.

So, when he came in, he took his shoes off and followed me upstairs to my bedroom. I turned on my lamp and told Alexa to play some smooth Jazz. Then I took off my robe and laid it across the chair and gave him the massaging oil from out of my nightstand. Then, laid down on my stomach with my arms and legs spread out. "I know I said these legs were not going to spread apart for him, but:

"Don't judge me; This One Is an Exception."

He started from the neck and then worked his way down to my back; I told him to stay right there for a moment because jogging on the treadmill really was working that part of my lower back. Shit! It was feeling so good I started moaning as if he were sexing me.

Stacey: Ahh, yes

He started working his hands down to my ass cheeks. Then it began to get really intensified with the way that he was massaging me. I could tell he was getting turned on by the way I was moaning with every rub on my ass. Because, when we were in a relationship, he used to turn the television or radio off just so that he could hear my moans.

However, most of the time, I would fake the moans just so that he would hurry up and cum. Although he's big, when the love and enjoyment are taken out of the equation, it just isn't pleasurable anymore. That's how the end of our relationship went. Why continue to give him the kitty-kat?

Well, when you're living under the same roof with a man who has bitch ass ways, you have to find some way to keep the peace; it just so happened that that was the way. So anyway, like I said, he was really turned on by the way I was moaning. Shit! That massage was feeling so fucking good. I couldn't help myself. He touched every muscle on the back part of my body, from the neck down to my feet.

Now, let's talk about the foot area. There are pressure points at the bottom of your foot that, if massaged right, you can have an orgasm. However, that would never happen because that's a skill that he wouldn't ever master. The moment that he touches me anywhere, the next step would be him fucking the kitty-kat with his tongue.

I could say the moaning noise makes him freaky ass shit, and I love it. I'll sometimes take it to a different level on purpose. Because, then, anything goes with him. It's like adding fuel to the fire. After he was done with my foot, he tapped me on my leg and said in a deep voice.

Steph: Turn over.

I turned over, and he started to massage the top part of my foot, then he lifted one leg up, putting my toes in his mouth, sucking on them, licking between my toes. It felt so good. He must have stayed on my foot for five minutes each before making his way up to my quads.

Then he rubbed my legs in a circular motion, going in and out, up and down my thighs, getting as close to my kitty-kat without touching it. Although my eyes were closed, I could feel the heat of his breath as his face sat over my kitty.

With a hard but quick blow, then a long but soft blow, he moved from left to right, covering my kitty, and then just soft and short frequent blows to put me in the right mood. I was ready. My body began moving from one side to the other, inviting his mouth on my kitty-kat. And then he pulled back and worked his hands up to my stomach and then to my chest, gripping them from the bottom cup and gently squeezing them, taking his index finger and rubbing my hard nipples.

I said to myself, "He knows exactly what he's doing." Again, I felt the heat of his mouth as he leaned over me. This time, slightly blowing on my nipples, and with the slightest touch, I felt the tip of his wet tongue as he licked the tip of my nipples. Oh, how he was more ready than ever to insert his dick inside of me.

How did I know it? Because I could feel his dick grazing across my leg, and it was hard as shit with no room for bending. I get it when a man refers to his penis as wood because wood doesn't bend.

I was like, "Damnn, all about now, this would be some awesome sex. But it's not going to happen." So, I pushed him off of me, and it took everything in me to do so. Then he said.

Steph: What are you doing? Let me finish.

Stacey: No, you're done.

Steph: Almost.

Stacey: Alright! But, you have to get off the tatas.

Steph: Why, you're getting horny?

Stacey: No.

"Knowing I was really lying."

Stacey: But you're trying to get me there.

Steph: Just let me finish so I can leave.

Stacey: The massage, right?

Steph: Yeah.

Stacey: Okay.

He's still leaning over me. He grabbed both of my wrists and then started rubbing up and down on my arms, working his way up to my shoulder, then around to my breast. Then he took his fingertips and began to rub down and around my stomach, then around to my sides.

Then around to my kitty-kat. As he gently rubbed my kitty-kat area, I felt his hot breath. This time, I wasn't expecting what came next, even though he fooled me last time by having me think that he was going to do one thing and kind of having me ready. Just for it not to happen.

But, this time around, I was surprised. "He's teasing me, okay? I like that; he just might get the kitty after all." With his mouth, he grabbed the lips of my kitty-kat and sucked on my clitoris. Moving his tongue around and around, up and down with the slightest touch. All I could say was:

Stacey: Oh Shit! Nigga you said just a massage.

My legs opened wider.

"Don't judge me. I know I said that I wasn't going to open my legs for this, but the tongue will make me do that because he's a hoover."

My hand went under the pillow above me and the other on his head, pushing him closer, fucking his mouth with my kitty-kat slowly, then fast, and with every stroke, there was a moan.

Stacey: Ahhh! Get it, that's right, get that shit, you know how I like it, don't you?

Steph: Too much talking. Shut the fuck up and cum.

The more I moaned, the more excited he got. Then he stuck his tongue inside of my kitty-kat, and I pulled my toy from under the pillow, turned it on, and put it on my clit. O M G, it really got more intense after that. It took me two whole minutes before I exploded all in his mouth and over his face.

Stacey: (screaming) SHITTTTTTTT!

Steph: That's right, give it to me, baby, hum, you taste so fucking good. This gonna be mine again. Nobody can make you cum the way I can.

I thought to myself, "Nigga stop talking before you bust my groove because that's not going down like that again." Now, ladies, when someone is giving you oral, we're no different from the men. If it's good, and I mean really good, your toes would start to point up towards the ceiling as you're having an orgasm. After that, he would have to get off of the spot because it becomes sensitive like a motherfucker.

But he just kept licking and sucking, and I kept pushing him away from me. I just couldn't take it anymore. Then he got up and started unbuckling his pants.

Stacey: Yo, what are you doing?

Steph: You know what I'm doing.

Stacey: Hold up! (The hand went up) You said massage, not pussy.

Steph: Girl, stop playing; you know you want this.

Stacey: No, I'm good; I'm ready to go to sleep now.

Steph: Come on, just let me get a little bit.

Stacey: There's no such thing as a little bit.

Steph: Well, just let me stick my head in it. Come on, baby, look how hard you got me.

Stacey: Damnn, I always make you that hard, don't I. But, you're only hard like that because your girlfriend didn't give you none. Shit nigga you came over here with a hard dick.

Steph: I don't have a girlfriend, nor do I want one. I should have made you my wife when I had the chance. Fuck it, you are my wife; we're just gonna get the papers so that it will be official. And there goes the bullshit again. He'll say anything to get the kitty.

"Why this nigga keeps calling me his wife? He had that opportunity and blew it."

Stacey: Says the man who has the stench of a woman all over him.

Steph: What, that's my daughter's perfume.

Stacey: Nigga whatever; I thank you for your service, and now it's time for your lying ass to leave; I have to get me some sleep now.

Steph: It's kind of late. Can I spend the night?

Stacey: Hell no. Now, come on, it's time to go. I have to work in the morning and you know you take entirely too long to get up and out in the morning. Shit! You can be late for work, I can't.

Steph: You can leave me here; I'll lock up.

Stacey: Nigga no, we tried that before, and you left my lights on and the water dripping. And besides, if you don't pay any bills here you don't get to stay here.

Steph: Damn, you really gonna treat me like that.

Stacey: Yes.

So I got up from the bed and escorted his mad ass to the front door, and honestly, I don't know why he's so mad because of three things.

I let him come over.

I let him touch me again.

I let him fuck me with his mouth.

Shit, he should be leaving happy as hell that I let him perform such good services like that.

"Don't judge me. He Turned Me Into This Person."

So, pretty much he got everything and more that he asked me for. So, he should be mad at himself for expecting the whole nine. After he left, I went upstairs to lie down because I was so tired, but my bed had a puddle of water on it.

Stacey: Damn! This shit feels like somebody turned on a faucet.

I got back up and changed my sheets, took another shower, and then went to bed feeling great.

Chapter 3:
The Day After

When 3 o'clock rolled around, and the alarm went off, I tapped the snooze button. Then it went off five minutes later, and again, I tapped it.

When it went off for the last time, I gave up and got up. I was so fucking tired I should have been drinking some Gatorade to replace the electrolytes that I lost last night after releasing so much of my bodily fluids.

Stacey: Shit! I have to get up and make my coins because a sister has bills to pay. Alexa, play Jay Z, "Fuck All Nite." As the music played, it gave me the energy that I needed to get my ass up.

I jumped out of bed and into the shower, brushed the chops, threw on the deodorant, and rubbed the body down with Vaseline.

"Ladies, men love women soft and clean." I put on my clothes and threw on a little perfume, a sprinkle here and a sprinkle there on the clothing, not the skin; it lasts longer.

Then, I went downstairs, made my smoothie, and went off to work.

I didn't see John today. I was really looking forward to smiling all in his face because of my sexual activities last night with Steph. But I didn't even get the opportunity to do so.

Fuck!

Later that morning, John ended up texting me, saying good morning and telling me to have a wonderful day.

I started moving my shoulders and snapping my fingers, just being happy that he acknowledged me today.

"Don't judge me; I like that type of attention. That's right, acknowledge me."

When you play the game, it can go either way. But because he texted me, that meant I was still in it. I also had five missed calls and three text messages from Steph. Like why?

Steph's text messages:

Baby I just want to say I enjoyed last night.

I called you, call me back.

I want to take you away all the expenses paid.

Why the fuck you're not answering my fucking phone calls or replying to my text. It better not be about another nigga.

Baby, please, I love you; call me back; I can be that guy for you.

Now, my thoughts on his text messages were:

Yeah, I know you did; I did, too.

I see.

You should have been doing that when we were together.

Okay, dude, now you see why I need you to take your meds.

And last but least, "FUCKING BIPOLAR."

Shit, I am not thinking about him. I got on with my day and took that ass to the gym. When I pulled up to the gym, who the hell was out there waiting for me?

That damn Steph, shit! He is so fucking irritating right now; I knew I shouldn't have ever let him back in.

Because now he's gonna be on some stalking shit again. Sitting outside my house, popping up at the gym, coming to the workplace, and calling me like fucking crazy.

Damn, I guess I bought this on myself. It's kind of worth it, though, cause he's a straight freak, and I love it.

"Don't judge me; that freakiness in him is serious."

So anyhow, I grabbed my workout shit, and I'm walking into the gym. And I'm trying to act like I didn't even see him sitting in his car waiting for me in the gym's parking.

And now he's calling me expecting me to come there to him. Shit, he got me messed up.

Steph: Stacey.

I kept walking; he got louder as he got out of the car to catch up to me. I could hear the door of his car slam shut.

Steph: Stacey, I know you see me sitting there, and I know you heard me.

I stopped at the door as he ran up to me.

Steph: Let me say some things to you.

Stacey: Really, like you could have waited until I called you back.

Steph: You know you weren't going to call me back.

Stacey: You didn't give me a chance to.

Steph: Stacey, stop playing games with me.

Stacey: What games am I playing?

Steph: You know what you're doing.

Stacey: No, I don't. Because I haven't lied to you about anything. I always told you the truth about how I felt. It's you who can't accept no.

I didn't take him inside the gym because he has no problem embarrassing me or making himself look like a donkey's ass.

Steph: Why are you not answering my phone calls or my text messages?

Stacey: Because I can't allow myself to get caught up in your web again.

Steph: Girl, you know that you still love me.

Stacey: I love you, but I'm no longer in love with you. I love you enough to say that I want you to be happy fucking this person and that person. I love you enough to set you free.

Steph: Well, what was last night?

Stacey: Shit! Last night was a good ass time.

Steph: It was more than that! You know it, and I know it. I had a lot of time to think about where we went wrong.

I thought to myself, "Okay, here comes the bullshit; this nigga is about to make me get loud with his ass, and I'm trying to keep my composer."

Stacey: What!! You mean where you went wrong? I was perfect in this relationship because I wanted it to work. You know, you're a straight asshole for even saying we to me. I put up with so much with you. And knowing the type of person you were when we were just fucking, I should have never made you my man. A fuck is all you should have been to me. So don't be trying to put that shit on me.

Steph: You're not perfect.

Stacey: (in a calm voice) I'm perfect for someone else I now know. I tried to be perfect for you, but that shit just wasn't good enough. I cooked for you, I washed your clothes, and I let you fuck me when you wanted it. You never had to worry about where I was or who I was with.

Steph: But baby, I had to grow.

Stacey: Nigga, don't hand me that bullshit; at 56 years old, one marriage, three grown-ass kids, and a 10-year relationship before me, you still didn't grow? And yet you decided to pursue a grown-ass woman in your childish ways. Like nigga, I'm a real woman doing real women shit. If you weren't ready, then you shouldn't have pursued me. You should have done what I'm doing now. Minding my own damn business.

Steph: What! You got it wrong. They say opposite attracts baby, and I see something in you that's good for me.

Stacey: Nigga, that's bullshit, it was the fucking shot.

That nigga started smiling from ear to ear as if he was getting ready to get it right here and now.

Steph: I'm not gonna lie; you do have a good shot.

Stacey: Listen, you're holding me up with this bullshit; I need to go get my workout in.

Steph: I'm gonna win you back.

Stacey: Don't count on it. You had almost nine years of my life; I know what dog shit looks and smells like to avoid it.

Steph: Watch baby, I'm gonna win you back; you always said that you were from the Show Me state, so let me show you. You said to know you is to love you.

Stacey: Boy, bye.

Okay, so that was enough of that bullshit, time to get this workout in. I just had to turn around and walk away from him.

Once I stepped into the doors of Planet Fitness, my mood totally changed because the peoples that work there are the fucking bomb.

They treat you like family, so fucking friendly and shit. I love the types of vibes they let off.

Angela: Hey, mama, I see you looking as beautiful as ever. How was work today?

Stacey: Good girl, now I need to get it in; you know my trip is coming up soon.

Angela: Girl, oh yeah, that's right, beautiful, go ahead and get it in.

Stacey: I'm trying.

Angela: No, mama, you're doing it, I see you.

Stacey: Thanks, baby girl.

As I was walking towards the locker room, I ran into my lil young bull, Mark, who works there.

Mark: Hey, you.

Stacey: Hey, how the heck are yah?

Mark: I'm good, you know this is my last week here.

Stacey: What! You leaving me?

Mark: Yeah, I'm moving on. I got a new job at a pharmaceutical company.

Stacey: Well, good for you, and congratulations, I'm gonna miss you.

Mark: I'm gonna miss you too.

O M G. I gave him a hug, and damn, his young ass felt so fucking tight and strong. In my head, I just started singing. "I want muscles, All, all over my body."

"Don't judge me. Most men that I've encountered in the past, as well as the present, didn't care about their bodies."

When I let him go, I just pulled my thoughts together and went on in the locker room and changed into my gym clothes. "Damn, I should have pushed up on that ass sooner; oh well."

I went into the locker room, took off my work clothes, and put on my sexy ass workout gear.

I also took the wig off and wrapped my head with my scarf, threw my things in my gym bag, locked it up in the locker, and now it's time to get to work.

Shit! It's Tuesday, and I'm feeling damn good.

Now, I would like to think that I'm known in the gym, because of how hard I would go on the machines.

And also have a cool attitude that would have motherfuckers wanting to work out next to me.

Because, like there's always someone that would come and work out right beside me watching, spying on me, and trying to challenge me.

Yeah, I know because I see them from the corner of my eyes. But what they don't know is that I'm really challenging them.

Like, don't come next to me and try to show me up, as if I can't keep up.

Shit, because you will surely have me twisted. I'm a competitive motherfucker, and plus this machine right here is what I do.

So, all that would do is just make me go in even harder. Sometimes, it brings me to the point that it's so hard for me to breathe, and still, I will not stop.

I would just slow down, get my breathing together, and then get back into it. You would be the one getting off first, not me. My competitiveness wouldn't allow me to stop.

"Don't judge me. You're the one that came over here challenging me and trying to make me look like I'm not in shape."

Now, for all my cardio people, I would like to ask y'all this question. Do you find yourself to be hornier after you work out, or do you find yourself tired?

As for me personally, I get very horny. As my sex drive goes to another level, when that happens, all I can think about is whose gonna be that lucky person.

Well! I know it's not gonna be Steph's ass for sure. I really want it to be John.

But that motherfucker still didn't hit me yet. I'm getting very impatient. I don't want to call him because it may seem like I'm being desperate.

And if push comes to shove, then I'll just pull out my vibrator, throw on Pornhub and just imagine Steph eating the shit out of my kitty-kat.

It doesn't make me cum, but it sure enough takes the edge off.

Therefore, motherfuckers won't be referring to me as a THOT (That hole over there) or desperate.

Shit, I think not.

That's why I'm just going to wait for him to call me. Damn! It's 7:30, and all I can think about is whether or not John's gonna call me.

I know I sound desperate right now, but I'm horny as hell, so there's a difference. Then what the fuck, my phone rings. Damn, it's that nigga John, "Yes, it's about time."

I pick up the call and press the phone against my ear.

Stacey: Hello.

John: Hey, what are you doing?

Stacey: On my way home.

John: Where are you coming from?

Stacey: The gym.

John: I already knew; I don't know why I asked that question.

Stacey: Right.

Then there was a pulse.

Stacey: Hello, you there?

John: I'm here, but I'd rather be there; what are you doing tonight?

Stacey: Oh nothing, going home to take my shower then get myself in the bed.

John: Do you feel like any company tonight?

I got really excited because this is what I've been waiting for. I didn't want to just come out and say it; I needed him too.

Stacey: Well, it all depends on how long it would take for you to get here.

John: Where do you live?

Stacey: I'm gonna send you the address

John: Okay.

I sent him the address, and when he checked, he said that the G.P.S. said that it would only take him 30 minutes to reach my home.

So, now I'm thinking like, "Damn, let me hurry up home so that I can tidy up the bathroom and my bedroom. Because I don't want him to think that I'm a dirty person. Mother always said that your first impression means everything."

The moment that I got home, I ran upstairs and told Alexa to play Jill Scott's "Is This the Way." As the song played, I cleaned up my bedroom, picked up the dirty clothes from off the floor, got the folding, and put away clean clothes that were lying on the chair.

Then I went into the bathroom, took the cleaning solution from under the sink, and got to spraying and wiping. I emptied the trash can, then took my shower and brushed my teeth.

With one finger, I stroked my kitty-kat to make sure it was fresh because he said that he loved to eat dessert before the main course.

Putting my finger up to my nose. "YES, just the way it's supposed to be."

Then I grabbed the lotion that I bought from Body Works and rubbed it all in between my thighs, on my ass, stomach, neck, and even my feet, just in case he has a foot fetish and decides to suck on my toes.

Then I went to the special drawer, pulled out those Victoria Pink Lace thongs that make my ass look eatable, and grabbed the bra that matched.

Now, ladies, if you are a Double D cup and the girls are not looking so perky, this bra right here is the truth. It will lift those tatas and make them look like you had a boob job and make the cleavage pop.

Five minutes later, my phone rang. It's John, I said to myself, "This nigga better not be saying he's not coming!"

So, when I answered the phone, I answered like I were ready for the bullshit.

Stacey: What's up?

John: I'm outside.

I started smiling, my voice changed, and I began talking a little more pleasantly.

Stacey: Okay, I'm coming.

I couldn't keep the smile off my face as I raced down the stairs, so ready for what was to come.

Chapter 4:
Let's Get It On

The bell rang again as I turned my ringer off and ran down the stairs, and all I kept saying in my Usher voice was, "It's on and popping; it's on and popping."

I opened the door, and he came in, but before he could get any further, my hand went up.

Stacey: Pump your brakes, dog.

John: What's up?

Stacey: Shoes off, please.

He looked at me like I was crazy and shit.

John: Damn!

Stacey: Yeah, I'm a little germophobic. Everywhere and everything that you stepped on would be transferred to my bed, if I let you walk around my house with your shoes on. My skin can't have that.

Then he went to sit down on my living room chairs to take his shoes off.

Stacey: Again, hold on, sit on the dining room chairs. Although your clothes is clean, you still was working in them all day. So, if I don't sit on my chairs in my work clothes, nor will you.

So, when I pulled out the chair, he sat there and started looking around. I'm looking at him and thinking to myself, "What the hell is he looking for?"

John: You have a very nice home. It's so cozy.

Stacey: Thank you.

John: Damn, you're looking good; turn around.

I twirled around as if I was modeling a new clothing line. Then I grabbed his hand, pulling him up from the chair so that he could follow me upstairs because for as horny as I was, I needed to cum so that I could go to sleep.

John: Damn, I guess we're gonna get right to it.

Stacey: I told you I have to get up early for work tomorrow, and I don't play about my coins.

As we're going up the stairs, he smacked me on my ass.

Stacey: Hum, harder.

He smacked it harder.

Stacey: Ouch, not that damn hard.

John: Well, you said harder.

Stacey: Did you see how big and thick your hands are?

John: You said harder.

Once we reached my bedroom, he started taking off his uniform. He took his jacket off, neatly folded it, and placed it across the back of the chair. Then he took off his shirt and repeated the same procedure.

I thought to myself. "Damn, a neat freak, I like it. I'm glad that I'm clean, or he would have a lot to say about me. But, hold on, he has a stomach."

Then he pulled his pants down, and again, I'm like, "Damn, what happened to his ass? Like he has none whatsoever. His ass is flat as shit, man!

I hope he could fuck, because most men that don't have an ass fuck, bring their whole body into it instead of working it from the waist.

This is definitely the 52-fake-out. His uniform hides all of his floss, making him look like he's a gymnast and even a bodybuilder." Damn! I was fooled.

He put his pants on the bench at the foot of the bed so neatly folded. Then, climbed into the bed.

He grabbed the extra pillow, put it under his head, and then started looking around the room. My thought: "Again, what the fuck is he looking for?"

John: I like the way you coordinated your curtains with the color of your walls.

Stacey: Thank you. I always wanted to be a home designer.

Then he picked up the remote from the nightstand and turned on the TV.

John: What brand of Television is this? It has a good sound to it.

Stacey: Samsung.

I reached over to him to grab the remote, and he raised his arm, holding the remote in the air so that I couldn't take it from him.

Stacey: Yo, what you doing?

John: Yo!!! I used to watch this back in the day.

Stacey: That's good, so you saw every episode, right?

John: Yup.

I took the remote and turned off the T.V. He looked at me like I did something wrong.

Stacey: House rules, my house, my T.V., my way.

John: Damn! Whatever happened to hospitality?

Stacey: You're about to be shown a lot of that.

I started kissing his neck; he just lay there. Then I worked my mouth down to his chest, and still no movement and no sounds.

So I took my hand and started caressing his testicles. He just moved my hand and put it on his dick, and still no movement or no sounds of pleasure.

It frustrated the shit out of me. Like five minutes done passed already, and still, he's not even hard. He must be a diabetic.

I felt like I did all this shit for nothing. I don't know why he would bring his impotent ass over here if he can't get an erection. Then this motherfucker says to me:

John: Can you suck on my dick? That will get me hard.

Stacey: Boy, hell no.

John: Why?

Stacey: Because you're not my man, and I don't go around sucking dicks. The kitty-kat's too good for that.

So, I just turned on the T.V. and laid my head on the pillow.

John: Why did you turn the T.V. on?

Stacey: Because there isn't nothing popping.

John: Because you still have your underwear on.

Stacey: You want it off, take it off. Or else it's time for you to go.

I just lay there watching T.V. and listening to my music being played on my Alexa Dot with nothing but disgust and disappointment on my face.

When he saw the type of expression I displayed, he decided to put everything into motion.

Deep inside, I felt as though he knew he wasn't gonna get another shot at this. So he started to do everything that I told him would turn me on.

He gently nibbled on my nipples while his hand caressed my kitty-kat.

Stacey: Ahhhhhhhhh

I started moving my body around as if I was fucking his hand. Not only did I get turned on, but he did, too. His dick started to get hard; my leg felt like someone was poking me with a stick. Yes, that ass is ready now.

He climbed on top of me and grabbed my legs, spreading them apart as he pulled my body closer to him.

He put my legs over his shoulder, and I felt the head of his dick as he was about to ram my kitty.

The hand went up again.

Stacey: PULSE!!!!! Where's the condom?

John: Oh, I don't like condoms; I like the natural feeling of a woman's pussy.

Stacey: Well, I don't like STD's

I reached into my nightstand, pulled out a condom, and made him put it on. I need to see what he's working with.

He was a little below average, but he was hard as shit. I hadn't had none in a while so it was fine.

Here we go again; he grabbed my legs and lifted them high, then worked his hands down to my hamstrings. He spread my legs apart and threw them over his shoulder again.

Then grabbed my waist and pulled me closer so that my kitty-kat and his dick will meet; then he inserted himself gently into me slowly, only giving me the head first.

Moving in and out, taking the head of his dick out just enough so that it would be touching the beginning of my hot pink tunnel, then sticking his dick back inside of me.

My mouth opened as I began to moan, looking into each other's eyes.

Stacey: Ahh...

John: Oh yes, you like that?

He slowly went deeper with every stroke.

John: Oh shit, you feel so fucking good.

Then he stopped just as I was about to have an orgasm.

Stacey: No! Don't stop.

John: I don't want to cum yet.

He pulled out and started nibbling on my nipples and rubbing around my kitty-kat. He had me moaning as if he were still inside of me.

I wanted him even more, so bad that I was getting ready to cum when he stopped again. He was really getting on my nerve with that shit. I was like:

Stacey: What the fuck!!!!

He stood over me once more, then jammed himself inside of me. I screamed.

Stacey: Ah!!!

It felt like he had grown, or my kitty-kat tightened up completely as if I was being broken into for the first time.

Damn, he was hitting it hard as hell; for every stroke, he went deeper into my kitty-kat; it felt so good that my orgasm was like the floodgates opened.

John: Oh shit, yeah, girl, let it go, give it to me, damn, I feel it, it's so warm.

He kept hitting it; he never stopped. But then, things took another turn. I stopped feeling him the way I was before I climaxed.

I guess his big ass used up all his energy fucking me all hard and shit. Then he gone lay his big ass on top of me, giving me a lazy fuck to the point that I couldn't breathe.

All I knew was that I needed him to get up. I put my hands on his shoulders, pushing him off of me, barely catching my breath.

Stacey: I can't breathe.

He just ignored me and kept stroking. I wasn't moaning anymore but gasping for air.

When he looked down at my face, I guess that's when he realized that he was too heavy for me and got up.

John: Are you okay?

Stacey: I, I can't breathe.

He then pulled himself completely up and flipped me around onto my knees fucking me doggie style.

The whole time that he was back there, I didn't feel him like that anymore. "Did he get soft or something? What happened"?

Although I had an orgasm, I needed about two more. Shit, I'm not done yet.

Stacey: Stop

John: What's wrong?

Stacey: I want to ride you, sit on the bench.

He sat on the bench, and I climbed on top of him, separating my legs, as I slowly inserted him inside of me.

Riding him slowly up and down at first, putting him deeper and deeper inside of me.

Until I began to ride him as if I was galloping on a horse. At that moment, I felt him again, and it felt good.

So good that I busted all over him again and again. After having several orgasms, he then busted. Then I got up.

Stacey: Now that's what I'm talking about. Okay, it's time to go to bed.

John: Damn, I feel like a $2 whore. You got your shit off, and now you're kicking me out.

Stacey: I don't know why you would say that because you got your shit off too. And plus, I wouldn't pay you for sex; that would be the other way around. Shit, you should be paying me for the cleanup.

John: What! It's your house, your bench, and your fluids, so it's your job. Remember?

Stacey: But you made me do it.

We both had to laugh at that one, I'll tell you. After he put on his clothes, he looked around on the floor and on the chair.

This dude made sure he left nothing behind; he checked and double-checked.

Then, after he left, I just waited for him to call. Like I knew he would.

But that was one hot night.

Chapter 5:
Bitch Ass Nigga

Question? How do you know when you have put it on someone?

They will text you or call you immediately after they leave.

You're being put on a peddle stool.

He can't stop talking about how the kitty feels.

Already making plans to do it again.

Claiming the kitty as his

Singing love songs.

At least for me, these things are how I could always tell if I left the man completely satisfied. Now, I'm just laughing because the very moment that he left, my phone rang.

I knew he was gonna call. I should have brought my phone downstairs with me because after going hard in the gym and then going harder with my ride game, running up the steps just wasn't in the script.

I'm like, "Dang, this nigga has me skipping steps to get to the phone. Shit! I'm bugging." When I got to the phone to answer it, it happened to be Steph.

Shit, all of that for him, oh hell no, he definitely doesn't get that type of energy from me.

Stacey: What's up?

Steph: Hey baby, I just want you to know that I love you, and I want to take you away somewhere.

Now, I just had a good night with John, and I'm tired, so the bullshit that Steph was talking about, I really didn't care to hear it.

Steph: Baby, did you hear me?

Stacey: I heard you.

I put my phone on speaker while I cleaned off my bench and changed my bedspread.

When I jumped into the shower to wash off the sex, my other line rung, and this time, it was John.

I started smiling and shit.

Stacey: Yo, I got to go.

Steph: Okay, I'll talk to you tomorrow.

Stacey: Maybe.

Steph: I love you.

Stacey: Whatever that means.

It was about time that this nigga called me because no one else other than Steph would be calling me, and I just hung up from him.

In my Jamaican voice. "Wah gwaan" I was cheesing hard. Because the very first time making out with someone, I would always get that call immediately saying how good it was.

"Don't judge me; I'm used to that type of behavior."

So when he made me wait until he got home, I was kind of nervous because I knew I put my thing down.

John: Hey beautiful, what are you doing?

Stacey: Laying down, trying to go to sleep.

John: Okay, I know you have to get up early, so I'm not going to keep you up. I just have a couple of things I want to say to you.

I thought, "Oh, I wonder what that is as if I didn't already know. Because the Kitty never let me down yet. "

Stacey: What's that?

John: Well, first of all, your shot is like that, and I want it to be mine. I'm a very selfish person, and I don't like to share.

Stacey: Well, you don't have to worry about that because I'm a one-dick-at-a-time type of person. I can't do multiple dicks in me.

John: That's good to know.

Stacey: Anything else, because I really have to get to sleep. You know I have to get up too early in the morning to be on the phone right now.

John: Yes.

Stacey: So, was that all?

John: No, we'll continue this conversation later. But for now, goodnight beautiful, see you tomorrow.

Stacey: Yes, handsome, see you tomorrow. Goodnight.

When we hung up from each other, I was like. "Shit, he better have reached out, or else there would have been some trouble, trouble, trouble."

I'm not gonna lie, though; I was getting kind of worried. I thought that he wasn't pleased, that's why he didn't call me right away.

Huh, there I go assuming shit.

You know, that's a serious problem I have because after I come up with my own assumptions, I tend to react to them.

It may not even be true, but it's true to me. So, fuck it, it's true.

That would be the act of a person who's always in her head.

"Don't judge me, Y'all Made Me This Way."

It's now Wednesday. I went to work, and it was actually a good day. I saw John, and he had Chocolates for me. I was like, "Damnn, he really listened to the conversations."

I wanted them, but I didn't want them because of my diet. Chocolate to me is like crack to an addict. You just want more and more.

And what makes it even worse is that it was a big bag of my favorite M and M's peanuts.

Shit, I took it anyway, though, by the end of the day, that bag was gone. Fuck, I just fucked up, so now instead of Friday being my cheat day with my ice cream drink made with banana, black bear rum, chocolate ice cream, peanut butter, and to top it off with whip cream on top, chocolate syrup, and a cherry it would have to be this.

And I would also have had some fried shrimp and French fries.

Damnn, I messed that treat up. Now, what am I gonna eat when my girlfriend comes through for our Friday girl's night that includes watching movies, drinking, eating, and talking shit about nigga's?

You know, before, when John and I were just talking, our morning hug was just a friendly hug, and now our morning hug is a sexual hug from the waist down to my ass, as he lifted me up, letting me know that he is a man in every way.

Holding me tight to the point, I'm like, "Damnn baby, take my breath away from me or go ahead and break a rib, why don't you."

However, knowing that he could lift me up made me happy because I always wanted to have this big ass held up in the air with my legs dangling as I'm holding on to a man's neck.

"Don't judge me. I saw it while watching Pornhub or a movie."

Either way, all I know is that it's one of my fantasies, and I hope that I can get that handled before I get too old because John appears to be such a strong man.

And I believe that he's going to be the one to fulfill that fantasy for me. I'm just gonna have to find a way to bring out the freak in him because he's a bit too laid back with his sex game.

Moving forward, every time that I've seen him coming up to me, this dude's facial expression was like, "If I could have it my way, I'll be in that kitty-kat right now."

It was crazy.

A week has passed, and now he's telling me that he needs it at least three times a week. Shit, I didn't want to say anything, but I needed it at least five times a week. Call me greedy.

"Don't judge me; I'm a female with a very high sex drive."

Stacey: Yeah, we can do that. But, I want, no, I need a couple of hours, not a quicky.

John: Okay, I'm gonna see if I could get a pill from my boy for Saturday.

Stacey: Saturday, seriously! Because you know what happened when we planned for a Saturday before.

John: Yes, Saturday, I promise.

Stacey: Okay, Saturday it is.

So, as far as I knew, all systems were a go.

When Saturday came, he called to confirm that we were linking up around 5 pm. I said to myself. "Okay, that's a good sign."

I got out of bed and threw my girl Jill Scott on. "Is this the way?" Went downstairs, got a bucket and cleaning supplies, came back upstairs, and started sweeping, wiping shit down, from the top to the bottom, until my whole house was clean and smelling good with Lysol lemon scent.

Then I went to the store and brought myself some more sexy ass underwear, then hit the gym.

After the gym, I had a protein smoothie so that I would remain light and energetic. Keeping my performance at ten.

Now, here's the embarrassing thing about this because: every time that I make my smoothie, I always put colon cleanse in it.

So, when he got here a little after six, the colon cleanse started working on me by giving me gas, and because I don't eat meat, it didn't smell coming out.

But when the gases start to flow, it can sometimes be loud. Then the next thing to happen is that I would have to take a shit, not a good feeling while being in the mix of things.

So, when we were having sex, I passed gas, and then I had to take a shit. I pushed him off of me and ran into the bathroom.

Sometimes, I wish my bathroom wasn't so close to the room. Because I was shitting and passing gas all at the same time, and it was loud coming out.

Although it's a natural thing, but why the hell would I take a colon cleanse the day of me hooking up with this dude? Like it could have waited until he left.

I felt so embarrassed. What a buzz kill! He wasn't supposed to witness none of that yet.

Although I washed when I was done when I went back into the room, he was sitting on the side of the bed with a soft dick; that only meant that he didn't get the pill, and all he was gonna do was give me a quickie.

So I was ready for him to go because I knew what the rest of the night was gonna be like: Me running back and forth to the bathroom.

Stacey: Oh, guess what? I'm good now, so you can leave.

John: I want to finish, suck my dick.

Stacey: Man, I told you before, I don't do that. And besides that, I have to work overtime tomorrow.

Which was a lie. I was just ready for him to go because I didn't want to feel any more embarrassed that I already am.

When Sunday came, we went all day without talking. Until the night, we conversated over text messaging. However, his text messages were coming in much faster than mines, so I started talking into the phone.

Now everybody knows that when you're texting, you're in control of the words you text. But when you're speaking into the phone as you're texting, your words don't come out the way you say them.

So, as John and I were texting back and forth, I had to speak into the phone to keep up with the pace of the text messages that he was sending.

I commented on something that he said, and then the texting stopped. I thought maybe his phone died. So, I thought nothing of it. I just said, "I'll see him tomorrow at work."

When Monday came around, I didn't see him, nor did I hear from him. Tuesday was the same, and I didn't hear from him. Wednesday came, and I still hadn't seen him nor heard from him.

So, I pulled out my phone and went to text him, and when I saw the last text message that I sent him, it said, "Sam,"

I was like, OMG, that's why he ghosted me because he thought I called him another man's name! It was supposed to be "Damn."

He knows I always say damn, shit, I say Damn to everything. And if he couldn't confront me for calling him another man, then he is truly a bitch ass nigga, so fuck him, and on to the next one.

His loss, not mine.

"Don't judge me; I don't have time chasing sensitive bitch ass motherfucker that can't say what's on their minds."

Shit, the sex wasn't like that anyway, but I would have just dealt with it until something better came along. Again

"Don't judge me; I think that I should have been born into this world a fucking man."

Now the drought is back on, and I'm back to using my sex toys and watching Pornhub.

Now I must tell you, my favorite thing to watch on that site would be "Threesomes." With two white women and a black man.

Because white women, I think, are at their freakiest with a big black dick. I know those screams are for real. Sometimes it almost makes me have an orgasm just listening to that shit, but I never do.

Because I be wanting to scream, but the walls are just too fucking thin, so I kind of hold back and just keep playing with myself until I just can't take it anymore, or I feel satisfied from the feeling of what almost happened over and over again.

Don't get it twisted; I may like to watch two women getting it on, but I will never let another woman do me.

I love hardcore sex, rough sex, and the feel of a man's muscles when I'm grabbing on him. To sum it up, I love dick.

However, right now dicks are not loving me. I have all of the wrong types of men approaching me. The type that's not even worth my time. Like I don't even know why these jokers would even think that they have a chance.

Speaking of jokers, wow, this nigga just won't give up with his confused ass. The whole time that Steph and I were together, He just couldn't get enough of one woman; he needed to have multiple women to fulfill him.

He kept sneaking and kept getting caught, "Now he's free, and he doesn't have to sneak around. He can have as many women as he wishes. But he keeps calling me up.

All I'm gonna do is let him take me out from time to time, spend his money on me, and let him eat me out when I need it.

"Don't judge me, He made me this way."

Shit, if he got tired of doing that, then he can leave me the fuck alone. In my Carly B voice, SCRAM!

You know, for someone who's never ever been by herself for a long time, this right here is a lonely world, and I don't like it.

I always prayed, "Father, I need a husband. Someone who will match my energy, someone I can trust, and who would love me the way that I do him."

One day, I happened to be going through my email when this dating website popped up that I joined 10 years ago. Me and my curiosity I just had to open it up.

Little did I know, to- And to my surprise, there were so many handsome white men waiting for me to respond. So, of course, the first thing that I would do would be to go through their profile to see their height, build, religion, education, age, and marital status.

But, fuck! They wanted me to pay for the membership now when it was free back then. Now isn't that some shit, I thought I was gonna snag me a white man.

The myth of white men not having big dicks is just a myth, because I didn't think that white girls would ever have big asses like black girls, but they do, so I just figured white men must have big dicks like black men too.

After dealing with King-ring-A-Ding and Steph, I was really ready for my white man to come alone, "A different flavor, so to speak."

"Don't judge me, Y'all Made Me This Way."

Chapter 6:
Meeting My Husband

So now I'm hanging out in the type of establishments that Caucasian men go to after work and during the weekend.

One day, my girlfriend and I found ourselves sitting at the bar having some drinks in a South Philly sports club when this handsome 6-3, blue eyes, blonde hair, built, well-dressed man, who was looking eatable in his white suit walked up and said in a deep voice.

David: Excuse me, ladies.

As he stood beside me. I thought that he was just coming to sit down.

David: I'm sorry for interrupting your conversation.

Then, his attention turns toward me.

David: But I just had to come over and introduce myself to you.

Stacey: Okay.

David: My name is David, and yours?

Stacey: Well, hello, David, my name is Stacey, and this is Trina.

He moved from my side and walked behind me to Trina's side to shake her hand. The way that she acted towards him was like, "You didn't see us talking."

She just looked at him and shook her head. I was so baffled because, for the life of me, I just didn't understand why she would treat my potential future husband like that.

I got a little upset with her, and looking at the expression on his face, I knew that he felt the type of energy that she was letting off, and so did I.

However, he just kept his cool and came back around to me.

David: So, tell me, Stacey, what are two beautiful women doing sitting here alone drinking? And what are you drinking?

Stacey: Well, first, we just needed to get out, and I'm drinking Long Island Ice Tea.

He bends over and then whispers in my ear.

Trina: Hold up; I know he's not trying to kiss you.

Stacey: Girl, relax! He's not trying to kiss me.

David: Well, I know if she didn't want to shake my hand, then she wouldn't want me to buy her a drink either. But, I'm gonna offer anyway.

Stacey: Awww, that's big of you.

David: Hey, I don't sweat the small things.

Stacey: Now that's what I'm talking about; I wish a lot of people in the world were like that.

I thought, "Damn, what a cool dude, because if she got like that with me. I would have been like, fuck you, now I'm gonna sit here, talk to your friend because I know I have her interest, and I'm just going to be buying her drinks for as long as she would have me and hope that she'll forget all about your evil ass."

"Don't judge me; you made me get like this."

But he was pretty cool about the whole thing. He told the Bartender, oh, I'm sorry, new age now, they're no longer called Bartenders, it's now Mixologist, and can you give them another of what they were drinking.

Then he shocked me by pulling out his credit card, giving it to the Mixologist, and telling her to leave this card open for the remaining night for me and my friend.

So yes, he now has my attention. I'm impressed.

Stacey: Are you sure about that?

David: Ms. Lady, I never doubt the money I spend on a beautiful woman.

Stacey: Okay then, thank you.

David: You are quite welcome. I'm going to go back to my table and let you and your friend continue with your night.

David walked away and went back to his table, and all I had to say after that was it looks like it's going to be a long night after all.

Trina: Girl, I hope you've not fallen for that bullshit.

Stacey: What bullshit?

Trina: Him leaving his credit card with the Bartender.

Stacey: What's to fall for? Everywhere we go, somebody always ends up treating us.

Trina: You know what he wants, right?

Stacey: Shit, I might want the same thing. But that doesn't mean that I'm going home with him. Listen, I'm going to need you to chill the fuck out and enjoy the moment.

Trina: I bet his card was either stolen, or it's going to be declined.

You know, I just had to laugh at her negativity, like she is really blowing my high right now.

Trina: Well, I'm going to pay for my own shit.

Stacey: Okay, shoot yourself. But if he's buying, then I'm ordering.

Trina: Don't order big.

Stacey: Girl, I don't like your energy tonight. Even if his card declines, I am more than capable to pay for my own shit.

As the hours passed, Trina and I sat there at the bar, talking, laughing, eating, and drinking until the night ended.

Stacey: Excuse me, excuse me, Ms. I'm ready to close the tab now.

Trina: Excuse me, but I'm going to cover my own tab.

Bartender: That's fine

I saw her throw her arm up, getting David's attention while I act like I didn't see that.

Stacey: Is everything okay?

Bartender: Yes, he has to come over to sign for it.

Stacey: May I see the receipt that he will be keeping and your pen, please?

She gave me the receipt, and I wrote my number on the back of it and gave it back to her.

Stacey: Can you make sure that he gets this?

Bartender: Yes, and your friend, how is...

Trina cuts her off.

Trina: Here's my coupon.

Bartender: Oh, I'm sorry, but this coupon ran out after 7: pm.

Trina: What! No, it didn't, and I was here before 7.

Bartender: Yeah, but you're closing out after 12: am; it's another day.

When David came up to sign the receipt, he overheard Trina and the Bartender. He assured Trina that he would take care of the bill for us. No strings attached, of course.

Trina: No, I'm cool; please don't get it twisted. I have my own money.

David: I'm sorry, I meant no harm.

I was like, damn, why does she always have to play that role? He was just being something different.

She pulled out her credit card to settle her portion of the bill, and as we were leaving, I went up to David, thanked him, and told him to check the back of his receipt.

David: Got it. I'll call you.

Stacey: Okay, and Thanks again.

David: No problem.

Then he winked at me with his cute self. Now, this was really a different thing for me because the brothers would buy you a drink, but they wouldn't leave their credit cards open for you to order whatever or how much you want.

Shit, I'm done with the brothers the white man just showed them up.

When Trina and I got outside, we departed ways; she went to her car and me mines.

I really hoped that David would call me because I liked the way he handled Trina's man-bashing ass.

Chapter 7:
His Situation

It's now 1 am in the morning and I'm just walking in the house when my phone rings.

Steph: Hey baby, I just wanted to hear your voice, I don't want nothing.

Then he hangs up.

OMG, this nigga must have been outside waiting for me to come home, stalking me and shit.

Steph, give it a break.

You know, for a second, I thought that it would have been David calling me. But then again, why would he be calling me this soon? It's not like he got the ass or something. All he did was spend some money on me.

However, as time went by, David and I talked on the phone almost every day, then it became every other day, then twice a week, to once a week, then three times a month.

We never again saw each other after that first night because, he was only here on business and lived on Staten Island in New York with a whole situation between him and his spouse.

Now, how did I find out about his situation? Well, every time we spoke on the phone, we always talked about seeing each other. So when he told me he was single. I said:

Stacey: I don't mind getting away for the weekend.

David: I don't either.

Stacey: So how about this: I'm going to my sister's house in Ohio; maybe I'll leave a day earlier so I can spend time with you before heading to my sisters.

David: Well, I'm going out of town, and I'll be flying from out of Philadelphia Airport that Friday evening. So maybe if I came down and stayed with you, we could spend the day together.

Stacey: But I already have Friday off, and I could take Thursday and just come up since you're leaving Friday; then I could continue my trip to my sisters and you to Philly.

Then he just kept insisting on coming to me, and that's when the red flags really started waving.

David: You know I would love to have you up here tapping that ass all over the place. But, you see, my ex and I bought this house together, and neither one of us is willing to leave right now.

Stacey: Oh, your ex, as in wife.

David: No as in ex-fiancé. We were going to be married, but she broke it off.

Stacey: So why still stay?

David: Because my money is tied up in it, and I really don't have it to leave and find my own. So, right now, this is what it is. And plus, I'm just trying to get my baby off its feet.

Stacey: Your baby?

David: My boys and I just started a company together, and it's in its first year.

Stacey: Oh! Okay, well I guess that I'll see you whenever.

David: Don't say that; I want to see you when I come back.

Stacey: When is that?

David: Monday Eve.

Stacey: Maybe.

When I hung up the phone from this Joker, and I do mean Joker. Because of this bullshit, he expected me to believe. All I could do was laugh.

Although David thought that I was okay with his situation, I really wasn't. Like Prince said, "I'm not fucking just for kicks." Well, I wouldn't have been fucking my potential husband just for kicks; I would have been fucking him with an agenda. So

SCRAM, deal with your situation and stop inviting people in it, you damn liar.

After that, I never called him again, and I stopped answering his calls. White boys have that nigga shit in them too. I tell you, these niggas read from the same damn handbook.

So, my days went on as usual. I did go to my sisters and enjoyed the company of my extended family. (My sister's in-laws).

We danced, did karaoke, drank, and played games. OMG, I had so much fun.

When Monday came around, my energy level was on zero from the lack of sleep, too much drinking, and too much damn fun.

However, I still was able to get a boost of energy to workout; as I went stronger into my workout, my energy level heightens until I got into the sauna. When that dry heat hit my ass, everything started relaxing. Shit! I don't even know how I made it home. It was all over.

Thirty minutes in the sauna may have been a little too much for me at that time. Especially when there was a lack of rest.

One weekend, my girl asked me about David because she thought every time I were on the phone, I was boo-loving with him. She knew that he lived in New York; however, she didn't know about his situation.

And I wasn't gone tell her shit. So, I just told her the long-distance relationship isn't for me.

One month has passed, and I swear, the hornier I've gotten, the more guys kept trying to get with me. It was like they could sense my hormones going crazy.

There were some young guys and some older guys. I was getting all types coming at me. If anything, I would have gone for the younger ones. You know, ladies, you can always tell when a man has diabetes, big ass guts and small legs.

That's not what I'm looking for; I need someone healthy and full of energy, I need that someone to match my energy in the gym and in the bed. Not the ones with the Erectile Dysfunction caused by Diabetes. Making you feel like it's your fault he can't get it up.

I can be a very greedy motherfucker, so don't shortchange me, or I will drop a motherfucker real quick. I like to fuck until I can't take it anymore.

Shit, it is what it is. And these unhealthy motherfuckers can't do that. In fact, there was only one motherfucker that could hang.

However, we don't get alone for shit. Like Mary J Blige said, "The Sex was good, you had my mind, and I let him come back every time." Shit that was a good song. But, like my man Teddy, also said: "It looks like another one, TKO."

Right now, the temperature's rising. I need someone from whom I could get it from when I need it. What I need is a freak because I can't stand boring sex.

You know, the boring type, lay down on your back, and let me get on top of you. Lay on your stomach, let me get on top of you, that type of shit. No foreplay, just in and out.

You know my girlfriend is always talking about her young lovers, but when I saw one of them, I was like, "Damn girl, how could you fuck that motherfucker? The dick has to be like, the bomb. Because he looks like WHAT THE FUCK."

But she would always say those, WHAT THE FUCK NIGGAS be hitting it right.

But for me, you have to look like something, like something has to make me want to open my legs to you.

And besides, I don't think these motherfuckers be pleasing her because when he leaves, another one comes right behind him. Shit, if you're still horny, it's time to invest in some sex toys.

Anyway, back to me, once again, the time has come when I get so fucking horny I'll start checking out the dick prints to see how big or how small it may be.

Rather, they're skinny, thick, or a normal width. I was talking to this cute 6'3 dude who looked like he was already hard.

I knew right then and there that he didn't grow that much more. Once he reached a full erection. I said to myself, nope, not my type.

Then I'm talking to another dude; he was an average height, 5'11, however he had no ass. I said not my type because when he fucks, he puts his whole body into it. He wouldn't know how to use his waist.

Damn, I need some. But, hold on, we're not gonna forget about the short men, that's 5'3 to 5'7. Ladies don't sleep on them niggas because big things do come in little packages.

"Don't judge me; I've been with just about every type of man to say that I know who has what."

It's either the kitty-kats the perfect size, or their package is huge. OMG. Screaming.

In my horniest state, who the hell would I run into. Nobody but my cute, short, and thick young bull. Every time I see him, DAMN! If only he were a little older.

Now tell me why out of all days, this dude decides to give me one of those; I want to fuck you hugs. And guess what? I gave it right back to him. Then he gone say:

Rich: We need to hook up sometimes, you drink?

Stacey: Hell Yeah.

Rich: What do you drink?

Stacey: My sweet drinks.

Rich: You like wine?

Stacey: Yeah, it's okay

Rich: Okay, maybe we can go over New Jersey to the Winery.

Stacey: That will be cool; I've never been.

Rich: Well, what you're doing Friday?

Stacey: I don't know; I play my Fridays by ear. Most of the time, my girl comes through.

Rich: Well, take my number or give me yours, and I'll call you later.

So I gave him my number, and he texted me his. Then, told me to lock him in.

Shit, he didn't even have to tell me that because I already know where it's headed. Of course, I'm gonna lock him in and hope that we link up soon.

Chapter 8:
My Young Bull

The next day, I received a good morning text with an emoji. When I saw it, it put a smile on my face because the text came in at 6: am.

Knowing that he doesn't have to be at work until 10: am that meant that he was thinking about me when he got up to go to the bathroom.

How sweet.

I'm not gonna lie; it did make my morning. It was good to know that somebody other than Steph was interested in hitting the skins.

You know, it's a damn shame, the things that you think about when you're approached by that certain someone that you really want or want to get with.

I mean, all damn day, I was thinking about how big he may be, how much energy he might bring, and whether or not he can eat the kitty-kat.

OMG, this young bull really made my day by reaching out. By the time I was done with work, we had texted each other several times, and before I got done with my workout at the gym, he would call me every day at the same time.

I guess that would be about the time that he was getting off of work. I was like, "Okay, he's showing initiative; he kept it going every day, the same routine."

Then, one day, he asked if I wanted to go out to my favorite spot (Las Margarita) on Friday night. At first, I said that I would go, but then I had to cancel.

I wasn't sure whether or not I wanted to fuck a young bull and especially someone that's around my son's age.

So, I told him a white lie and said that I was watching my grands this weekend. It was so cute that he seemed disappointed when I canceled our date, but oh well.

"Don't judge me, Nigga's who kiss and tell made me this way."

Now get this: even after I turned him down, I knew eventually that I was gonna link up with him. I just had to see what type of young bull he was.

Throughout numerous conversations that we had, he never once made me believe that he was one of those bitch ass niggas that like to gossip because those types are the worst kind.

So, it was refreshing to know that he wasn't one of those dudes that would brag on his dick or his fuck game to his boys. In fact, he never brought up sex in our conversations.

He played his shit just the way it was supposed to be played by trying to get to know my likes and dislikes, past relationships, future plans, and even my concerns.

He had me believe that his maturity was much more than what I expected. So, now I can see why men my age and up act the way that they do.

Hun, they're trying to keep up with the young bulls because women like me want a man without all the bullshit, like:

1. Wife issues
2. Baby mama drama
3. Erectile dysfunction
4. Lack of energy
5. Playing childish games.

So, the third time he asked me out, it was to come to his place for some drinks and conversation.

Now ladies, my mother always told me that YOU NEVER go to a man's house on the first date. You always meet in a public place. So, this is the way the night went when he called:

Rich: Hey, I'm on my way home. Can you be here about 8: pm?

Stacey: Yeah, send me your address.

He sent me his address, and when 7 pm came around, I started to get myself ready.

I waited for the very last minute to take my shower since I now knew that we lived so close to one another. Then, I threw on a pair of my Victoria's thigh-high yellow laced panties that covered only the front of my kitty-kat, and the silk portion of it was just the string going in between my ass and around to my waist.

The bra that came with it was also yellow. The front of it is lace, cut to bare most of my breast and just covering my nipples with the silk scraps on the back.

Then I threw on a pair of tights that I would generally work out in, that pulls everything together, and a sweatshirt that I bought from Gucci.

But, hold up, let's not forget about the smell goods. A little dab in between my thighs, a little on my wrist, and a little behind my ear.

As I was getting ready to walk out the door, my phone rings.

Rich: Where you at?

Stacey: I'm on my way, man.

Rich: Okay, call me when you get outside.

Stacey: Cool.

The moment that I hung up from Rich, Steph called me asking what I was doing tonight.

I told him that I was going to Ron's Jamaican Restaurant to get me a small Jerk Chicken platter, then I'm going back home to have myself a movie night. He asked:

Steph: Can I come over and keep you company?

Stacey: No, not this time. I had a hard day at work, and I need some alone time. Just me, myself, and I.

Steph: I can help you relax.

Stacey: I'm good, maybe next weekend. I just need this time for me right now.

Steph: Okay, call me if you change your mind.

Now, I didn't foresee that in my tonight's plans, so there's no chance in hell that's gonna happen.

When I pulled up to Rich's spot I shot him a text, then waited for him to come to the door before getting out the car.

Because this January cold is not playing around tonight, it's cold as hell out here. When Rich finally came to open the door, he had on ball shorts with no damn underwear on; his dick was just jangling.

I was like, "Damn! This nigga might hurt me." As I entered the door, he gave me a quick hug.

Rich: You smell good.

Stacey: You do, too.

It was good to know that he believed in washing his ass and putting on the smell goods for a woman because the older men just don't. I think that the older guys just don't give a fuck. Like take me as I am or don't take me at all.

Once I got all the way into his apartment, I saw that he does hookah. I thought to myself, "Damn, this nigga gonna have some kind of breathing problems and won't be able to perform. Shit!"

He asked if I did Hookah. I told him no. So, he took a couple of puffs, then he said:

Rich: I got some Margarita mix in the kitchen. You can make it yourself so that you won't say that I'm trying to get you drunk.

Stacey: But, I'm the guess.

Rich: You are indeed; I don't want you to think that I'm gonna try to take advantage of you, so if you get drunk, it's not my fault.

Stacey: Okay, cool.

Rich: But, first, I want you to taste this brand of Tequila.

Stacey: They have different brands?

Rich: Yeah, in fact, grab those shot glasses after you're done making your drink.

Stacey: Okay.

Rich: Did you eat? I got us some Party Wings.

Stacey: I don't eat meat, and besides, it's too late.

Rich: I said I was gonna stop eating late myself.

I made my drink and brought the shot glass to him. "Ha, he's not trying to get me drunk, hun." The lies he told. He filled the drink all the way to the rim. After we did the first shot, he said:

Rich: Let's do another.

Stacey: Cool.

We did, and instantly I started feeling it. Now, the type of music he was playing was a little too slow for me, that it started relaxing me too much as I started yawning.

Then, he asked:

Rich: What type of music do you listen to?

Stacey: I'm an open book when it comes to music; I like all types.

Rich: Well, what type of music do you prefer to listen to?

Since I've been on this Afro beats lately, that's what I told him I wanted to listen to. Because he seriously needed to step it up a notch.

That slow, old-school music was putting me to sleep. When he put on my Afro beats, that shit put life right back inside of me.

I started singing and dancing and shit. And when my song came on, it was on.

Stacey: This is my song, "Joanna Jo Jo Joanna".

He just sat back in the chair and watched as I damn near danced and sang every song that was played.

Rich: Oh, that's how you be in the club?

Stacey: Hell yeah, when I have my drinks in me, it's on and popping.

Rich: I see you.

Then I started drinking the drink that I made for myself, and I guess it put me in another world because I was gone.

All I knew was that the chicken he was eating started to smell really good, and I was ready to dig in.

What stopped me from doing so was the weight that would have come with it.

"Don't judge me; the mirror made me like this."

Chapter 9: Drunken Love

Once all my dance songs went off, I sat my ass down and sipped more of my drink. That's when the deep conversation started.

Rich: So why would a beautiful woman such as yourself be single?

Stacey: Because niggas my age and up are trying to act like young dudes.

Rich: I got that; how many kids you have?

Stacey: Enough to the point I don't want anymore.

Rich: Do you have some home with you?

Stacey: Nope, they're all grown and on their own.

Rich: That's what's up.

I said to myself: "Okay, small talk."

Stacey: I am really feeling these drinks right now.

Rich: You want another?

Then he gone get his light skin up and grab the bottle and sit it right on the table.

Stacey: No! Are you trying to get me drunk?

Rich: No, I'm not. So, tell me about one of your sexual experiences.

Stacey: What you mean?

Rich: Have you ever had a Menage-a-trois?

Stacey: Why would you ask that?

Rich: Because I want to know. You look like the type that would have had one.

Stacey: What!

Rich: I ask because most women I know have had one.

Stacey: And you just thought I did?

Rich: Yeah, because you don't seem like you're the boring type.

Stacey: You're right about that assessment; I'm not the boring type. But I hate the fact that I can't tell you that I've never done that. Even though I wouldn't call it that, I would call it a Menage-a-tweet.

Rich: Why would you say that?

Stacey: Because my old boyfriend back in the day hooked me up with one between him and his Spanish friend of my choice, of course. Jose! I would never forget him. I had such a crush on him when I first saw him until I had him. His friend was this cute Spanish guy who owned his own bar in Kensington. He had a nice built and plenty of mussels.

Rich: Were you nervous?

Stacey: Hell yeah.

Rich: Tell me, how did it go, I want details.

Stacey: Okay, so when we went to Jose's spot. We talked for a while until I thought I was ready. But still, I couldn't do it. Now, don't get me wrong, I did pick him because I thought that he was cute and all, but I didn't feel anything for him that would make me want to open my legs when the guy that I have feelings for is right here. So, how do you prepare yourself for that? With plenty of drinks. Because I started to have a change of mind, so my dude told Jose.

Rich: Hold on, was this the any random person?

Stacey: No, silly, one of his friends, I already told you that.

Rich: Okay, continue.

Stacey: So, he told Jose to go get a bottle of hypnotic because that's what I drink and that it will relax me. And he did; he went downstairs to his bar and brought up a bottle and set it in front of me with a glass then told me to go for it. Then the both of them went to take a shower. I heard them talking in the shower; I was ear hustling, because I wanted to know what was my man's thoughts about this.

Rich: What were they saying?

Stacey: Jose didn't speak English too well, so he said it in Spanish; I understood what he was saying; I speak it a little. He was like: "Hombre, estas jodidamente loco, por muy buena que sea, desearia que otro maldito hombre tocara a mi mujer.

Rich: English.

I started laughing because I would have thought Rich had some Spanish in him; he looked like it.

Stacey: Man, you're fucking crazy; as fine as she is, I wish another mother fucking man would touch my woman. And my dude was like, "We made a deal that we will give each other a Menage a Trois, but it has to be one of my friends, and it would be one of hers." Jose was like Ella me Eligio. Guau! Me siento honrdo. (She picked me. Wow! I'm honored.) So anyway, while they were in the bathroom, I damn near drank the whole bottle. When they came out some 15 minutes later, my dude took my hand and brought me into the bedroom and undressed me, then started eating me out. OMG, that nigga was the fucking bomb with that shit. I used to call him a human Hoover. That motherfucker had me looking forward to that shit when he said he was coming over. He always had me climbing the fucking walls. Like this nigga used to come over to my house every morning after I dropped my kids off to school just to eat me out. And get this, he was living a whole other life.

Rich saw how I was getting turned on just by telling him that.

Rich: Come on, you doing too much reminiscing. Come back to the story.

Stacey: Okay, damn, but how can you ask me about sexual experiences and not expect me to reminisce when you had a motherfucker that did the shit that turned you completely out?

Stacey: So, he has me on my back, legs so far apart, and he's working the hell out of his thick ass tongue. And again, he had me backing away because I couldn't take it. So, he grabbed my legs and held it so I couldn't move. Then his friend came in and started sucking on my breast. I wasn't really feeling it because he wasn't doing it right. I needed to feel teeth, just enough to get me excited about what we're doing, or shall I say, what I would allow Jose to do.

Okay, so then he turned me over and started licking in between my ass, and his friend got under me and started eating me out. That was another failed attempt. Like damn, this nigga, I picked the wrong motherfucker. I should have picked his other friend, who has a foot fetish. At least the toes would have been all in his mouth, every last one of them. Shit he probably

Would have made me have an orgasm.

Rich: Did you suck his dick?

Stacey: Whose?

Rich: The bull that climbed under you.

Stacey: The Spanish bull? Hell no, I wasn't feeling him.

Rich: Did he ask you to?

Stacey: Yeah, but no. So, when I turned over, and I witness the dude putting on his condom to fuck me, his dick looked small as hell while he was hard. Listen, it wasn't like my dude had a big dick because he didn't. He was a little below average, but it fitted just right. So, now you know that Jose really wasn't working with shit. After that, I was ready to go home because I was disgusted. As a matter of fact, I was disgusted and disappointed with everything that was associated with this. Like, I wasn't happy at all. I was drunk, and I started crying because, now, I felt dirty as hell, and I couldn't believe that he would let another man touch me like that. Especially after he flattened my tires because he thought I was out cheating on him with another man. After hearing a message on the answering machine that this guy left me.

Rich: The type of answering machine that was like a tape recorder?

Stacey: Yes, I tell you, those things were worst then the damn cell phone.

Rich: So why didn't dude call your cell phone?

Stacey: Because my dude provided me the phone that he controlled so that he could keep tabs on me. And every time that he was mad at me or couldn't reach me, he would get it turned off. So, the only way that I could receive my messages for sure was through the landline.

Rich: I get that. But how was he able to check your messages?

Stacey: Because I was with him for 3 years and I gave him the okay to come and go as he pleased. Whether I was there or not.

I started shaking my head.

Stacey: Bad mistake man, bad mistake.

Rich: No shit.

Stacey: Are you gonna let me finish telling you the story or what?

Rich: I thought you were done.

Stacey: Almost. So, when I got home, I took a long hot bath. By the time I got out of the bathtub, my skin was smoking from the heat.

Rich: Damn!

Stacey: Yeah, because I just felt so fucking dirty and ashamed. I must have stayed in the bathtub for at least 30 minutes, letting cold water out and putting fresh hot water in. By the time I got out of the bathtub, my skin was smoking. Shit, I was really in my feelings that day, crying and everything. I think he heard me because when I came out, he did make it all better.

Rich: That's what's up.

Stacey: I'm not gonna ask about your story because I know you have a lot of them.

Rich: You already know.

Stacey: But, fuck it. The type of person that I am, please tell, indulge me. But hold up, I don't want to hear about your experience with a young chick. You said that you like dealing with older women, so I want to hear about the first older woman you dealt with.

Rich: Well, the first O.G. that I was with was married. I was around 25 years old, and she was 47. Her husband was a Cop, and she was a Homemaker,

Stacey: What, you're bold as shit.

Rich: Yeah, I used to go to her crib every other day.

Stacey: And where was her husband?

Rich: He was at work.

Stacey: Shit.

Rich: So, I would enter through the basement door and nobody couldn't tell that I was going to her house because she shared the back entrance with her neighbors. And check it out, she would always be in a house dress with nothing on underneath.

Stacey: Easy access.

Rich: Right. Soon as I would come in, she would start pulling my pants down and sucking my dick. And when she sucks the dick, she likes to take the whole thing; I tell you, this O.G. was a real freak.

Stacey: Damn.

Rich: She would get me so fucking hard, then tell me to fuck the shit out of her. And every time that I was about to cum, she would take me out of her and start licking on the balls until I calm down. Then she'll start sucking me again to get me hard. Then she'll put a sock in her mouth and bend over and tell me to go in her ass. I was like, shit. Man, I fucked the shit out of her ass. That bitch was screaming and everything. At one point, I thought I was killing her. She didn't want me to stop, either. Now get this: like I said, this was every other day I did this. The same routine every fucking time. Until one day, her husband came home early.

Stacey: Oh my God, did y'all get caught?

Rich: Nah, she didn't even want me to stop because he did the same thing every time he came in the door. That motherfucker would go straight upstairs and jump in the shower. Not a hello or anything. She said that he was fucking someone else, so she's gonna get her shit off too.

Stacey: So, wait a minute, y'all never stopped.

Rich: Nope, she wanted me to keep fucking the shit out of her until she bust

Stacey: Did she use a toy on her kitty?

Rich: Naw, she played with it with her fingers.

Stacey: Damn,

Rich: I kept fucking her until she had an orgasm, and then I nutted all in her ass. She said that was the only way that her husband couldn't tell that she was with someone else. Yo, I love older women because y'all are straight freaks. But, fuck that, I had to leave her crazy ass alone before she gone and get my ass killed.

Stacey: Right.

I took another sip of my drink and then started dancing again.

My African music was popping. I was whining, dropping that ass on the floor and everything.

When I turned around and looked a Rich, he was so turned on that he pointed his finger out, telling me to come over to where he were sitting on the couch; with this, I want to fuck you look.

I went over, and he pulled me on top of him with my legs wrapped around his, facing him face to face.

The hardness of his dick against my kitty-kat was making me so wet as he grinds on me; we're moving our body to the slow beat of the music as if we were dirty dancing on the floor.

Then he grabbed both of my breasts, bringing them to his mouth and gently nibbling on them with his teeth as he continued to grind that hard-ass dick against my kitty-kat.

I was ready. He had me moaning as if he were inside of me, stroking me slowly. I wanted him so desperately and deeply inside of me that my kitty-kat started jumping.

He slipped his hands underneath my shirt, working himself up to my breast, uncovering my nipples.

Then he grabbed one of my boobs with his teeth and put it in his mouth, sucking and nibbling while massaging the other.

He had my kitty-kat throbbing strongly with anticipation. I got up on my knees, grabbing his thick ass head and licking it. Then, whispered in his ear:

Stacey: I want you to fuck me now.

Rich: You ready?

Stacey: Fuck yeah, I need it.

Rich: You sure?

Stacey: Yes, give it to me.

He then pulled my shirt over my head, taking it off. Then he lifted me up off of him and pulled down my pants.

Then gently laid me on the floor as he climbed over me. He started nibbling on my legs as he worked his way up to my kitty-kat, spreading my legs apart, sucking on my clitoris, pulling it, then taking his tongue and licking it with such pressure.

"Damn, this young bull got skills." I almost had an orgasm right there on the floor, and he didn't even have to give me the dick.

Then he kissed up the center of my belly to my breast, putting them in his mouth, then up to my lips.

As he began kissing my lips passionately, he stuck his big fat juicy dick inside of me. And I grabbed hold of him, holding him tight.

It was one of those Rick James songs. "It was pain before pleasure."

Stacey. Ahhhh.

Rich: Damn, girl, you're so fucking wet.

Then he took himself out of me and stuck it back in. But this time, going deeper.

Stacey: Ahhhh

Rich: Damn girl, this pussy feels so fucking good.

Then he came out again and stood up, then pulled me up.

I tell you, the liquor really had me done to the point that standing really wasn't an option for me at that time.

Rich: Come on, baby, let's go to the room.

He grabbed my hand and, directed me to his bedroom, and sat me on the edge of his bed.

I was completely naked. Now for the life of me, I didn't even remember him taking his clothes off.

When he walked up to me, his dick was right at the level of my mouth.

Rich: Go ahead, suck on it.

Stacey: That's not my thing, so if it's not done right, don't blame me.

I put the head into my mouth and started sucking it until my mouth started to feel tight. Which wasn't long; OMG, like, what the fuck! I can't believe I just put his dick in my mouth. Shit! That damn liquor.

I started to lick the head and the side of his dick while massaging his testicles.

He was hard as a brick, so hard that I could feel the veins popping out.

"Damn, I'm getting even more excited just seeing this."

Rich: Ah, that shit feels good.

"Don't judge me for someone who's not a dick sucker, watching Pornhub schooled me on some things."

He then pushed me back onto my back forcefully, grabbing my legs, pulling me towards the edge, throwing my legs behind my head, and ramming his fat, light dick inside of me.

I screamed a loud scream.

Stacey: Aww!

He was fucking me as if he were just released from prison. Like if this were the first kitty-kat he had in years.

I screamed so loud I think the whole apartment building must have heard me.

I couldn't hold it in. It felt like he was in my stomach. I begged him to stop.

Stacey: Rich, Rich, stop, please, you're hurting me. I can't take it, please, please, it's too much.

Then he came out and started sucking and licking on my kitty to calm me down because I was so damn loud, or maybe because I said he was hurting me.

Either way, it did. Like I couldn't hold it in. This young motherfucker feels so good. "Damn!" I was having orgasms back-to-back.

Then he stuck his dick inside of me, and I could feel my kitty tightening up, gripping him.

And again, he was like a hammer hitting the walls of my kitty. I just couldn't take it, and again, I was screaming.

I started tapping out, hitting his chest, and pushing him, trying to pull him away and out of the me.

But the more I tried, the harder he went. At this point, I knew his neighbors had to hear us. Correction me.

This nigga had my ass in tears. Then he came out of the kitty and started licking and sucking on me again.

Stacey: Aw, yes, yes, yes, yes, that feels so good, please don't stop.

Rich: Cum again, I want to taste it.

His tongue was feeling like my vibrator 10 times stronger. Not only did he have a thick dick, he had the tongue to match.

"Damn, what the fuck is this young bull doing to me."

I couldn't take that anymore. I started moving backward away from him; he grabbed my ass, pulling me back into his mouth.

Rich: Where you going? Stop running; this is what you wanted, right?

Stacey: I, I can't take it.

Rich: Yes, you can. This is what you wanted, right?

Stacey: Yes, but I can't take it.

He didn't stop licking and sucking me. I grabbed his thick bald head and started pulling him into me even more as I fucked his mouth. And when I got ready to cum:

Stacey: I'm cumming, Rich, I'm cumming. Oh, my Gah.

Now, I know I should not be calling out God's name while I'm having sex with a man that is not my husband.

So, I cut myself off from completing the word.

Stacey: I'm cumming, Yessss!

I wrapped my legs around his neck as I'm squeezing his head, pulling it into me while releasing all of me in his mouth.

After I was done, I thought to myself: "Damn, he's a fucking freak, I love it."

Then he turned me around on my stomach, laying me on the edge with my knees pressed against the frame of the bed.

And with his hands placed on my ass. He opened me up and jammed his dick inside of me once more. And I screamed.

Stacey: Ahh, shit.

I felt every inch of him down to his balls slapping against my kitty; he had me in tears.

I was crying because it was hurting so bad at times, then at other, it just had me moaning because it felt so fucking good.

All I knew is that he was just too fucking big to be rabbit fucking me like that, I would have thought that my big ass would have stopped him from going so far inside of me, but I didn't.

I could feel him in my stomach. I was screaming. I had enough. He was hitting it again so good that I started cumming.

Now, in all of my sex sessions, I can count on one hand as of to how many men made me cum from hitting it doggy style.

I came so hard that all my energy left me. I dropped down to the floor on my knees, and the funny thing about that is that he never missed a beat; he dropped down right alone with me.

Still inside of me fucking me. "Damn."

I stayed wet the whole time. We were fucking for more than 2 hours. This young motherfucker was really giving it to me.

Then he started fucking me faster and even harder. Like damn, I didn't know that he could move so fast. He started moaning and saying:

Rich: Damn, your pussy is so fucking good, I can't hold it anymore, I'm ready to cum.

Stacey: Come on, baby, give it to me.

As he started to cum, he gripped my hips so damn tight that he left marks of his fingerprints on my skin.

And with a loud voice:

Rich: Fuck!

After that, I knew that he had ejaculated because when he was done, he attempted to stand up.

He couldn't. He just fell right back down on me, then started kissing me on my neck and licking me up and down my back. Then he said:

Rich: Are you okay?

Stacey: Yes

Rich: Come on, baby, get on the bed.

He helped lift me up from the floor because I was so drunk.

As we laid in the bed, facing each other, he on his side and me on my stomach, he began to rub my ass in a circular motion.

Rich: Damn, girl, your ass is soft.

Stacey: Shit, your dick is so big.

We started kissing passionately as if he were going away for a long time.

The longer we kissed, the more he started to squeeze my ass.

Then he got up and climbed on top of me and stuck his dick right back inside of me.

Even though I was still so very wet, it felt like we were just fucking for the first time.

Damn! I just put my face into the pillow and screamed. Then he said:

Rich: Arch your back for me.

I got up on my knees and arched my back.

Even though I didn't want to, because I knew that I would feel him even more inside of me.

I was just a little tired from all the screaming from the first time.

But this time around, I think that he wanted to take it a little more easier on me.

Because he proceeded to give me slow but steady strokes, taking time out to enjoy the kitty,, feeling every part of me,, hitting my G-spot just right. While scratching up and down the center of my back lightly as he was stroking me. My ass was twirling on his dick, throwing it back to him.

Rich: That's right, girl, throw that ass back.

Stacey: Ahh, yes, I'm giving it to you. Take it.

Then I started to bounce up and down on his dick, still moving slowly, feeling all of his thickness, taking it a little deeper inside of me because I was ready to cum. My voice raised.

Stacey: Oh shit, Rich, Rich, I'm cumming.

Rich: That's right, come on, girl, give me that warmness.

He then stopped stroking me and just stayed there, still inside of me, having me to decide how much of him I wanted, giving me full control.

At times, there were slow strokes with him just hitting my G-spot, then I would take him in a little more, bouncing harder and faster, just as I got ready to cum again.

Putting him all the way inside of me until it started to hurt. Then I would back up and just feel the head as I would bounce my ass up and down on him, slowing it down once more.

At this time, I wasn't screaming; I was moaning moans of pleasure. This fucking young bull is turning me the fuck out right now.

Damn! He's really on some experience shit. After I came for the 4th time of the night, that was completely it for me.

I just dropped down on the bed with my arms spread out and my legs still open.

And yet this dude still followed me down to the bed, stroking me. Laying all that thickness on top of me. Then he said:

Rich: Turn over.

As I was turning over, he helped me. Shit, I guess I was moving to fucking slow for him.

He climbed on top of me and started to stroke me. Giving me all of him. I screamed.

Then he came out again and put one of my legs in between his and one on his shoulder, turning me on my side.

Going so deep in me, I swear this young bull was making a new hole in me. I started hitting him.

Stacey: Stop, Stop, it hurts.

Rich: I'm getting ready to cum.

I knew then, at this time, if I wanted more of him in the near future, I would have to just take it at this point and let him have his way until he bust.

Rich: Ahhh, Ahhh, I'm cumming, Shit, Ah fuck.

And at that time, I couldn't even be mad because we bust together. He made me feel so fucking good. Like, I really needed that. And I didn't feel ashamed about it. That's right. I'm gonna sleep damn good tonight.

Don't judge me; good sex will have you like that.

As I got dressed to leave, I turned around and gave him a kiss, and our kiss wasn't just any kiss.

It was a goodnight, you were fucking awesome, and we're definitely gonna do this again type of kiss.

Stacey: I want more of you.

Rich: You can have more. Shit! I want more of you! We're definitely gonna have to set something up.

My thought was, "Oh my God, I can't believe I said that. And in the same token, I'm glad that he said it back."

I tell you this much, though: I didn't feel the need to go home and play with my toy. He left me completely satisfied.

"This young bull got me hooked." OMG, I'm officially a cougar.

Chapter 10: The Aftermath

When I got home, he texted me to make sure I made it there safely because I was intoxicated. I thought that he was a gentleman for that.

I jumped in the shower smiling because I couldn't remember the last time I felt like this, and it was all because of him.

The next morning, when I woke up. I received a 6 am text from Rich, saying that I drained the shit out of him and how tired he felt.

Also, saying that I have some good-ass pussy, and he wanted more.

I smiled because all I kept thinking was these young girls maybe younger than me. But, I bring a little something extra to the table than they do. Called experience.

"Don't judge me for being a cougar; you old motherfuckers made me this way."

Now everything changes because we had sex. Like a typical dude, the calls stop coming in on the daily.

However, I would get a text every 4 days saying that I want to see you. Like a horny woman, or shall I say a woman that's getting good dick and not wanting it to stop, I would answer it.

Like, what the fuck, I wish I was fucking this person and that person. Because, if I were, that shit wouldn't even fly with me.

I have this rule, one dick at a time.

And plus, the convenience of us living so close, were that it was very easy to just stop everything that I was doing to run to him, get my shit off, and come back home, was fucking awesome.

Shit, it was like, I'm going to the store, I'll be right back. Hun, his young ass didn't even know he had me.

I remember one conversation we were having, and he called me a player. I guess he thought that I was fucking everything that moves.

Until I told him my one-dick-at-a-time rule: if I'm giving myself to you, it's only to you. So therefore, there would be no issues because I would hate to have to kill a motherfucker just in case the condom breaks.

And another thing, don't make me wait long to see you because I don't like that.

He just looked at me like this bitch making ultimatums. So, we got a quicky in, and I would go home, or he would go home.

After that, I would hear from him every 3 days to link up.

The following week, which happened to be Valentine's Day. I didn't even hear from that motherfucker.

My thing with him was, you don't have to be in love with me, to let me know that you're thinking about me.

All my other dudes hit me up to say happy V-day, and what makes it worst is that I haven't even fucked them, nor do I have any plans of doing so.

Steph ass even made time to take me out to dinner, knowing that his ass wasn't getting none of the kitty.

So, do I feel some type of way about that bullshit? Absolutely yes. It made me think, if I'm gonna put myself through this shit, I may as well be with Steph cheating, lying ass.

At least he will come and take me out to different places. For instance, on Valentine's Day, we went to this nice restaurant in downtown Philly called The Capital Grille.

One thing I can say about Steph is that when he's saying forgive me, he would go all out for me.

But I'm not a material person. I just want him to be true to me.

So, anyway, it's Valentine's Day, and we're at the Capital Grille. Now we all know that on days like that it would be crowded.

So, when we walked in, he holds the door open for me and the young ladies with the na-booty (big butts) and big breasts, showing all the cleavage.

Don't get me wrong, I'm not jealous; I'm just hating a little because I wish I had big tits too.

I get that he's a gentleman, which is why he held the door for the young ladies as well, so I didn't get mad.

However, as they walked passed him, his eyes got stuck on their asses.

Disrespectful; this is one of the reasons we're not together now.

So, I didn't say anything to him about that because, after all, he's not my man anymore. We're just going out for dinner.

Now, it was a bit of a wait for a table after checking in. So, I just stood by the doors and waited.

Steph: Baby, they said it's gonna take about 15 more minutes before we get a table.

Stacey: Ok, that's cool.

For every female that was dressed as if it was summer and had a big ass, his head turned every time they passed him.

Like he wasn't even low-key about it, now, it's getting on my nerves. Because I knew I was looking good with my leather tights, a silk red shirt that hugged my waist, showing a little cleavage, and my high-heeled shoe boots.

I wanted to be like in my Tubac Voice. "Nigga All Eye's On Me." Or my Aretha Franklin, "R E S P E C T, find out what it means to me, just a little."

But I chilled and just let it ride. Before you know it, 15 minutes came and they called this group name. Four guesses that followed the waitress back; when Steph saw that, the nigga in him came.

He was like, hold the hell up. So, he walked over to the Concierge's desk.

Steph: So I see that you just called some people, and we were here before them.

Concierge lady: Sir, they had a reservation.

Steph: I have one too.

Concierge lady: What's your name?

Steph: Steph.

Concierge lady: Sir, I can see that you're next. However, you can sit at the bar if you can't wait.

Steph's voice became bombastic.

Steph: If I wanted to sit at the bar, I wouldn't have made a reservation, don't you think?

I just looked at him, shaking my head.

Concierge lady: Sir, I see that your reservation is for 2, and theirs was for 4, so they received a table that seats 4, and you will receive a table for 2.

Steph just turned around and walked away; I thought, "Wow, IGNORANT."

Stacey: Why you always have to act like that?

Steph: Like what? I made a reservation, and they just came in and got a table before us.

Stacey: But you were really rude just now, and you didn't have to be.

Steph: Look, baby, I brought you here for dinner and good conversation, so just let me handle the other things.

I just started singing my Kenny Roger's song in my head. "You got to know when to hold them, know when to fold them, know when to run away, know when to hide."

Stacey: Okay, cool, sorry.

So, I just shut my mouth because it isn't like anybody else stepped up to the plate and said, Stacey, I want to take you out today.

No more than 3 minutes later, the waiter called his name to seat us.

Now, the funny thing about this is because where we were standing, the table was empty the whole time.

Boy-o-boy, did he fuss about that. I felt so embarrassed; I was hoping that there wasn't anybody in this restaurant that knew me.

In honor of the special day, I let him be the man just to see how well he knew me. I let him order the drinks as well as the food.

I must say, he did very good. The drink he ordered was a white Zinfandel, and the main course was a Chicken Marsala.

I thought to myself, "So, he really has been paying attention."

Then, we started having a general conversation. And for the life of me, I tried my hardest to stay away from the past us topic. Because every time we will talk seriously about us, it almost always ends with an argument.

So, the way that he started the conversation was like:

Steph: I hope that you appreciate me bringing you here because this restaurant isn't cheap.

Now, how the hell am I supposed to respond to that?

Hum, "Nigga! Don't say that. You act like I can't afford to feed myself. Girl, just smile."

Stacey: I do appreciate it. Thank you.

Steph: Baby, we can do this at least once a week if you give me another chance.

Stacey: I don't know about that because you destroyed every little trust that I had for you.

Steph: Come on, baby, I'm trying.

Stacey: If only you tried harder when we were together instead of running with those other women, we wouldn't be in this position now. But I can tell you this much, though. I'm not mad at you anymore.

Looking at this fool with a big-ass smile on his face, assuming that he has a shot was pathetic.

Stacey: Stop smiling, all the shit you done to me. You turned me into someone that I never thought I would be.

Steph: What's that?

Stacey: A cougar.

Steph: What! You're fucking someone?

Stacey: Yes.

His whole expression changed after that.

Steph: Then why you're not with him tonight, why he's not here?

Stacey: Because you only wanted me and not him.

Steph: You know what! Enough of that; let's change the conversation.

Stacey: Okay! How was your day today?

He looked at me like he really didn't have any words. When the food came, it was just on time because we ate, then we left.

He asked did I want to spend a night at his house that night, and I told him no. When we pulled up to my front door, he said.

Steph: I know you're not going to invite me in.

Stacey: You're right about that.

Steph: Why are you playing games?

Stacey: Whose playing, I'm dead serious.

When I got ready to get out of the car, that motherfucker kept his ass right in the driver's seat.

All that being a gentleman went out the door since he wasn't getting no ass. Oh well, who fucking cares.

Chapter 11:
Lesson Learned

Sunday rolls around, Monday comes, Tuesday hits, and then Wednesday morning, I get a text from Rich saying:

Rich: Good morning, beautiful.

For the life of me, I tried not to respond because I was still mad at him for not giving me the recognition on Valentine's Day, so I didn't.

Then, later on that day, he texted me again saying.

Rich: Mean lady, why are you ignoring me?

So, I figure that it's time to take this young bull to school and let him know some things.

Stacey: What! At this time, I don't have any words for you.

Rich: Why? What did I do?

Stacey: You know you don't have to love me to say Happy Valentine's Day.

Rich: Sorry, let me make it up to you.

Stacey: Okay, but I wonder how.

Rich: I need you to see me tonight. Can you come over?

I went, but when I got there, he had red roses sitting on his coffee table. I just knew they were for me.

It kind of change my whole mood with him. So, we started tonguing each other down.

I took off his shorts and worked myself down to his dick as I scratched down his back all the way to his ass, kissing him and nibbling on him.

Rich: Aww, yes, baby.

Then I took my tongue and licked up the side of his dick until I got to the head.

Then I put the head in my mouth, sucking it as if it was a lolly pop, with one hand massaging his balls and the other rubbing up and down his dick.

Rich: Aww shit.

I couldn't do it long because my mouth started tightening up. So, I started licking around the head.

Once my mouth loosened up again, I put it back into my mouth and tried to take it all until I started to choke.

Then, I just went up and down on it. The reaction that I got from him made my kitty-kat jump.

Like damn, this young bull is the only one that made me be like this without being drunk.

Stacey: I'm done

Rich: Turn around and get on your knees. You know how I like it. I want to see that big ass.

I did, and he grabbed my legs then, put them around his neck, and started eating me from behind.

I came instantly; then he gently put my legs down.

Rich: Stay there, don't move.

I didn't, and he inserted himself inside of me. And I screamed. I swear, every time we have sex, it feels like the first time.

Most of the time, he had to stop because he said I was screaming like I was in pain. Shit, you think?

He was fucking me as if he was hitting it for the first time, plus he has a mandingo dick.

Most of the time, our sessions would last 2 to 3 hours, and he would have climaxed about 2 times and me 4 to 5 times.

But because we were giving each other a quicky, it didn't last long. Nor did we have that many orgasms, and when we were done and I was leaving, he never gave me the flowers.

So, as much as I love fucking and sucking that big dick of his, I have to leave him alone. Because he's selfish, inconsiderate, and full of shit.

If he didn't buy these flowers for me, then he either bought them for someone else or someone bought them for him.

Either way, the dick-sucking stops, the fucking stops, fuck it, it all stops.

Because I'm a selfish motherfucker for the person I'm fucking. I don't like to share at all.

So, before I left, I gave him a passionate kiss and then said:

Stacey: I can't fuck with you anymore.

Rich: Why?

Stacey: Because you have that young bull mentality.

Rich: What you mean?

Stacey: Let me put it to you this way. You like the kitty-kat, right?

Rich: Hell yeah.

Stacey: You like the fact that when you call, I come, right?

Rich: Yeah.

Stacey: So why couldn't you think of me on V-Day?

Rich: Because you said that we're just fuck buddies, and nothing couldn't come out of this.

Stacey: I don't care what I said to you; still, you could have picked up the phone, and not only that, but I can't be sucking you and fucking you and you're fucking someone else.

Rich: Han!!!!

Stacey: And on that note, I'm out.

So, I left.

The whole time while driving home, I was like, "Damn, I'm gonna miss that shit." In less than 24 hours, my ass was super horny and wanted to be penetrated.

So, I got into my car and drove out to the county to a sex store that stays open after hours just to buy a dildo.

Yo, I was tripping doing so shit like that, even when I don't use the inserts. When I got there, the damn store had closed down.

"FUCK!"

Now, I want to call this motherfucking young bull so bad, but I'm not gonna.

Right now, Steph's tongue with my bullet is looking really tempting.

I thought that when women get over 50's, their sex drive is supposed to slow down.

Whatever doctor researched that theory should have asked me because mine is through the roof.

Chapter 12:
The Reunion

Two weeks done passed, and this nigga didn't call or text, and right now, I'm just going cold turkey with no inserts.

My bullet is kind of sort of taking away the feeling though, because I have to turn it up to the highest level.

It's now three weeks, and I've been hitting the gym harder than ever, trying to get my mind off of this boy's dick game.

And in the course of all that, I lost 18 pounds, and I'm looking and feeling good as shit.

Right now, I'm looking so good that I can have my picks of who I want because the men are coming at me hard.

I was passing out my number to men that I thought can give me the type of work that I needed and so wanted.

Looking through my phone to see which one can I call for tonight, and damn, I forgot my girl called me like a day ago.

Let me call this chick and see what's up for the night.

Stacey: Hey girl, what's up?

Trina: Nothing much; I got us 2 tickets to a fish fry for tonight; you down?

Stacey: Sure, I'm not doing nothing.

Trina: Okay, it's from 9:pm till 1:am. I want to leave my house at 8:pm so that we could get a table.

Stacey: Okay, cool, I'll be there.

Trina: Okay, see you then.

At first, I was like, "Damn, what am I gonna wear?" I went to my closet and just stood there looking at my dress pants and jeans.

I have jeans that I bought too small on purpose, still with the tags on them. I pulled out a black pair of Gucci jeans that I bought on sale from Macy's.

"Let me see if I could get my big ass in these yet." I put one leg in the pants and pulled it up, and it went up past my thighs.

"Okay..."

Then I put my other leg in and pulled it all the way up without no problems.

"Damn..." I rushed to the hallway mirror to see how they looked on me, and I was completely satisfied by what I saw.

"Damn, this workout is working."

I turned around and looked at my ass in them. "And the ass is popping."

Now I just had to find a nice shirt to wear. "Oh, I got it."

I looked all around in the dresser drawer for my black and white button-down shirt that I also bought at Macy's.

Threw it on and didn't even have to wear a belt.

"Okay, I guess black and white is what I'm sporting today."

Then I put on my Gucci black boots that Steph brought me because I caught his cheating ass, so I could stop being mad at him.

"Oh, well I mind as well go all out and be Gucci down tonight."

So, I pulled out my black Gucci bag and my 3-quarter length Gucci jacket and took another look in the mirror at myself, twirling.

"She looks like money." Then I left to go over to Trina's house.

By the time I reached Trina, she was already in her car waiting. I parked then I got into her car.

Let me tell you a little something about my girl, Trina. She's been my girl for well over 30 years, and I love her like a sister.

Like everybody, she has her issues that she struggles with, and sometimes she tries to pass them off on me.

For instance, every man is a cheater, a liar, or have some kind of issue. When she would give a man another chance, she would try to convince me not to.

Sometimes, I just think that she wants me to be alone like she is.

But I don't want to be alone, so in order for me not to let her in my head, I would only tell her what I want her to know.

Nothing more or nothing less.

So once I get into the car she immediately asks me about David. "Like, damn girl."

Trina: So, how are you and David? I haven't spoken to you lately, so I suspect that the both of you are hitting it off well.

Stacey: No, girl, I told you that I can't fuck with him.

Trina: Why?

Stacey: Because he has a situation at home.

"Now, why the hell is she smiling hard? What type of shit is that."

Trina: I knew something was up with him.

Stacey: How? From him spending money on me or trying to treat us?

Trina: Yes.

Stacey: Girl, please. Something always has to be up when a guy approaches me.

Trina: It is, and you know it. All they want to do is hit.

Stacey: Well, he wasn't even talking about hitting; we spoke about a lot of other things.

Trina: Oh, so what happened?

Stacey: Well, he lives in a home with his ex-fiancé and her mother. A home that they both are buying with the expectancy that they would be married by now. But wait, before you even respond, he also said that because he and a couple of his friends are starting their own financial company, his money is kind of tight. So he can't afford to move out at the moment. So he just moved to another room.

Trina: Do they have any kids?

Stacey: Yeah, he has 3 by her and another by someone else.

Trina: And where is his company?

Stacey: In his garage.

Trina: Girl, that's bullshit.

Stacey: It's all bullshit to me. That's why I'm not dealing with it. However, I have been getting me some young dick, and girl, OMG, he has it going on.

Trina: And who is this one

Stacey: Damn girl, you're saying that like that's all I be doing. Like I'm some kind of hole. He's a young bull that I know.

Trina: Who?

Stacey: You don't know him, but here's a picture of his light ass.

Trina: He's cute and thick.

Stacey: Yes, girl, so is the dick.

Trina: Girl, I'm jealous.

Stacey: Why, as much as young bulls, you be fucking.

Trina: Shit, I didn't have none in a minute, I'm going through a drought.

Stacey: Well, I hope that you get some real soon. Cause I'm enjoying this one.

Trina: Well, welcome into the cougar world; we must toast to that.

Stacey: Definitely.

Then, I was interrupted by a phone call.

Stacey: Oh, that's my young bull now.

Stacey: Hello.

Rich: Yo, what's up?

Stacey: Nothing.

Rich: I'm tryna come see you tonight.

Stacey: I'm out now, but call me around 10:pm

Rich: Okay, answer your phone.

Stacey: I will.

After we hung up with one another, Trina gave me this look. I just ignored her because I wasn't about to feed into her shit.

Now we're at the fish fry and just about everybody that was there I knew. Once again, the drinks were coming left and right.

It really was one of them nights for a good time. Every time someone came over to the table to talk, I introduced Trina.

And every now and then, she would engage in a conversation, and then, there's other times when she would just put that same look on her face like, "I'm ready to go."

So, when I was asked to dance, I asked him to ask one of his friends to ask her so that she can start having fun, too.

But, damn, the person that she was dancing with was one of my old flings. I wanted to say something to him, but they seem like they were having a good time dancing the night away, so I just left it alone.

After the drinking, eating, and dancing were done and, it was time to go. Eric and I were standing by Trina's car talking.

Now Eric is the guy that I was dancing with when Trina and James came out of the bar.

They were hugged up as if they knew each other for a long time. Then, when they reached the car, James took his arm from around Trina's neck.

James: Stacey?

Stacey: J-money? Oh my God.

I acted like I didn't even know who he was when I saw him dancing with Trina.

We gave one another the biggest hug. I think we both were surprised to see each other, him more than me, because, I was already surprised when I saw him dancing with Trina.

Damn, that hug made me think of the one-night stand we had years ago.

James: Damn baby, what's going on. It's a surprise to see you here.

Stacey: Right, but it's more of a surprise to see you here. What you're doing here.

James: Hanging out with the boys, what about you?

Stacey: You know me, still looking for my boo.

James: You still look tasty.

Eric: Yo Jay, chill the fuck out, that one's mine.

James: I will not; this is the one that I let get away.

Eric: One man's trash, another man's treasure.

I'm just listening to them and laughing at how they're fussing over me. It's cute, though.

When I turned around to Trina, she was getting in the car.

Trina: Girl, I'm ready to go.

Stacey: Okay, here I come.

Now, what I'm looking for is a money maker, someone that isn't cheap with the coins and have plenty of stamina.

I know James is that dude, but his friend, I don't know. And then again, James, don't hang around broke nigga's either.

So, before I got into the car, I gave James my phone number and told him to call me sometime.

Not considering that I just gave his friend my number first before we came outside. "Damn, I'm being a little messy right now."

Eric's dancing was turning me on, not to mention he's tall, built, and have a cute smile. His voice is deep, and his lips are very suckable.

I would love to know more about him, but after giving James my number, it may have sent the wrong signal.

Eric may not even call after that move.

Damn.

Because I really don't like to move backward, but it seems that's all I've been doing lately.

"Don't judge me. I sometimes think with my Kitty-Kat."

When I got in the car with Trina, she was looking some type of way.

Stacey: Yo, it was such a surprise running into James. We hooked up once, and I wanted him to be my man. That nigga had energy like I've never had before.

Trina: Damn girl, is there anybody that you didn't fuck.

Stacey: Yup, your dad.

I could tell that she was back into her funky mood, so I said nothing else to her.

We just listened to the music until we got back to her house.

I got out of her car and got into mine. I told her that I'll talk to her later, and she said okay, with sarcasm and I paid it no mind.

So, I was like, "Whatever."

When I looked down at my phone, I could see that Rich called me a couple of times and also sent me a couple of text messages. One of the text messages said: "Where ya at?"

Although I wanted to get my freak on tonight, it was too late to call him back because I knew he had to be at work too early.

So once I got home. I took my shower, got in the bed, and pulled my vibrator from under the pillow.

Put on some Pornhub "big dicks" and went to work thinking about the last time James and I were together.

I didn't have an orgasm, but it surely did the job of taking the edge off.

"Don't judge me; I did what I had to do."

Chapter 13:
Never Letting Go

As the days passed, I didn't hear from Rich. However, I did prove myself to be right about Eric; he didn't call me at all.

Honestly, I think as they were riding home, James probably threw salt in the game. If so, I only wish that he showed that much initiative after our first rendezvous.

After that night, I heard from James every day, sometimes twice or more. We had a lot to talk about.

In one of our conversations, he told me that he was mad at me when I told him that I got married the following year after hooking up with him.

For the life of me, I didn't see why would he be mad; he didn't want a relationship because, if he did, then he would have pursued me.

So, oh well, life goes on. He told me that I'm not freaky enough for him and that I should watch Pornhub to see how women get down on there. Shit, now that I remember, that's how I was introduced to Pornhub.

Shit, I was like, "NIGGA SCRAM." Because you just insulted me. You don't get everything at once; you have to work your way into it.

Now, two weeks has passed, and James wants to get together.

The following week, when I had time, we did meet for some drinks on a Friday eve. He kept ordering me drink after drink, assuming that my legs would open for him so damn easily.

Listen, one thing for sure, two things for certain, I do know what I'm doing when I'm drunk, and if I wanted to give him the kitty-kat, then he would have gotten it.

He didn't have to get me drunk at all; the only thing that he had to do is hit the fucking Mega Millions.

Lol, I tell you, this nigga was doing everything he could to get me to that point.

When he dropped me off, he wanted to come in. And if I didn't want to take it slow with him this time, I probably would have invited him in. Because after having my drinks, plus having him stimulate my mind with good conversations, it had me wanting to be stimulated in other ways.

But, to have another hot, one-night stand with him was like out of the question. Because If I were to give him another shot, this time around he would have to work for it.

Shit, this body now moves in ways that he can only imagine.

However, he will get a point for being a gentleman, walking me up to the door, and not trying to come in unless invited. I liked that.

Yes, that night, he scored a brownie point.

Once I got into the house, I just laid across the couch because, I couldn't make it up the steps. I was done, trashed.

Then, I received a text from Rich.

Rich: Beautiful, what are you doing?

Stacey: Laying on the chair.

Rich: You feel like some company?

Stacey: I feel like a massage.

Rich: Can I come over? I'll give that to you.

Stacey: Only if you know what you're doing.

Rich: I do.

Stacey: Okay, come on.

By the time Rich came to the house, I was completely out of it. I had unlocked the door then, stripped down into my panties and bra, and went to sleep.

Just to be awakened by a loud banging noise at the front door. "OMG, who is it?" I totally forgot that Rich was coming over.

Rich: Rich, open the door.

"What the hell is he doing here?"

Stacey: What's up?

Rich: Open the door.

Stacey: Wait a minute.

I couldn't barely get up. I went to open the door, "OMG, I never locked the door?"

When Rich saw me, he was like, "Damn girl." I went and laid back on the chair.

Rich: Okay, I'm not gonna say anything; I'm just gonna give you your massage and let you sleep.

Stacey: What are you talking about?

Rich: You said you needed a massage.

Stacey: Nigga, that was yesterday. But, since you're here, okay then.

So, I'm on the couch lying on my back when he came over and started to massage my feet. In my sleepy and drunken voice:

Stacey: Please get the ball of my foot. I realized that those skinny hills on my boots weren't made for the type of dancing I was doing.

Rich: What? You went out tonight?

Stacey: Yeah, I went out with an old friend, and I had way too much to drink.

Rich: That nigga was trying to smash.

Stacey: I know, but that wasn't happening.

Rich: Because you have me for that, you better not give my shit away to nobody else.

Stacey: You mean my shit.

Rich: Whatever, Stacey, don't play with me.

"Is this nigga for real? Is he really acting jealous right now? What a fucking joke!"

After that, he said nothing else and just massaged the shit out of my foot.

He was doing a damn good job too. Sticking his fingers into the ball of my foot. Oh, his hands felt so strong.

He was giving me exactly what I needed. Then he started rubbing up my legs, massaging my calf. Going up and down just in that area.

Stacey: Awww, yes.

Then he worked his way up to my thighs again, rubbing it up and down with the palm of his hand.

Then he went into my inner thighs and spread my legs apart. Rubbing up and down, working his hands to my Kitty-kat, rubbing it in circular motions.

OMG, I'm getting that feeling that I want to be penetrated. But I'm so done.

Stacey: What are you doing? You said massage.

He still said nothing as he moved my panties to the side. I had to open my eyes to make sure it was him and not James.

Because, out of all the times Rich and I messed around with each other, he was never quiet, and he never gave me a massage, either.

Then he started eating me out.

Stacey: Oh yes, Ja-

Damn, I almost called him James, I wonder did he notice that shit, even though it didn't stop him. He just kept going.

But, hold on, I've never had sex on my chairs. However, this would have been the first time because I didn't want him to stop.

I must say, every time he's eating me out, it's like he's getting better and better. A professional even.

This motherfucking young bull revived the shit out of my ass; it was like having a cup of Espresso with a Red Bull or a Monster drink added to it.

Now, I have to do something with this energy.

Stacey: Move.

I started pushing his head away.

Stacey: Move.

He got up.

Stacey: Take off your pants, then sit on the chair.

Rich: You sure?

Stacey: Just do what the fuck I said.

And he did.

When I looked down at his dick, he was already hard as shit, so I didn't have to do anything else but climb on that mountain.

When I put him inside of me and started riding him, I was definitely in another zone. I was fucking him like I was a professional rider.

We both were moaning, then I wanted to tease myself and make him feel even better, so I started riding just the head of his dick. Using my legs, going up and down on him. Shit, this is what the gym workout is about.

It felt so good that I started cumming. In a soft voice:

Stacey: Ahh, I'm cumming.

I threw one finger up.

Stacey: That's one.

I knew if I stayed on top of him, I was gonna start having multiple orgasms.

I didn't even care about the work that I would have to do the next day with getting my chair cleaned.

I just was cumming all over the place.

Stacey: Yes, Yes, that's two.

He grabbed my waist and slammed my body down on him as he pumped back.

After I'd had several orgasms and was really ready to go to sleep, I started hearing noises from my chair as if we were breaking something.

Then it happened again.

Stacey: I'm cumming again.

He started pumping faster. I could feel him in my stomach.

Stacey: Ah, yessss, that's four.

I could feel my kitty-kat tightening up on his dick.

Rich: Fuck girl, that's some good ass pussy, you feel so fucking warm.

He lifted me up off of him, standing me up on the chair, putting my kitty in his mouth, gripping my ass cheeks pulling me into him.

My hands went flat on the wall as if I were Spider-Man, ready to climb that motherfucker.

Stacey: Oh My Goodness.

I'm moaning. The more I moaned, the harder he was sucking my kitty and the stronger his tongue felt on me.

Stacey: I'm about to cum.

Rich: Come on, I want you to cum in my mouth.

He took his finger and, inserted it inside of me, and started wiggling it. It felt like he inserted his dick.

That's how tight my kitty gotten. With his mouth on me and his finger inside of me, I lost it.

Stacey: That's five.

He sucked what little energy that I had in me out. I was done; he helped me down, then put me on my knees, stuck his dick inside of me, and started hitting it hard.

I was screaming.

Rich: What's my name?

Stacey: Rich.

Rich: What's my name?

Stacey: RICH. AWWWW!

Rich: Remember that shit. Don't you ever call me another nigga's name.

Stacey: I didn't. ahhhhhh, you're hurting me.

This nigga was ripping a new hole in my kitty because I almost called him another man's name.

Shit, I didn't think he heard me. He had me slapping the back of the chair, and every time that I would move my body forward, taking him out of me, he would grab my waist and bring me right back to him and go right back in. He was giving me angry sex. Like my man, Kevin said: Fucking pineapples. Or my nephew would say: No, no, noo.

Stacey: Rich, it hurts.

Rich: I'm getting ready to cum.

I tried to take it just a little more, but it seemed like it took him forever to cum.

I couldn't take anymore. My screams got louder.

Stacey: Ahhhhh, Rich, please, please, I, I, I can't take it. It hurts so bad.

Rich: I'm cumming, Ahhhh, shitttttt.

He took it out and was cumming all over my ass. After he came, he stood back and almost fell.

I was left on the chair with my face in the pillow, trying to recoup. The way my kitty-kat was feeling, I didn't believe it was casual sex.

Yeah, it may have started out like that until I called him someone else. Because he was fucking me like, "Yeah bitch, you been keeping my pussy away from me, you know I need this shit. Then you gone call me another nigga too, motherfucker. You had another nigga hitting my shit. That's why you called out his name. Now I'm gonna fuck the shit out of you."

Okay, so nigga, you can't be hitting my kitty-kat like that. Trying to fuck my shit up so the next person wouldn't like it.

Then to make matters even worst, this motherfucker knocks my cycle on. The next day, my cycle came on.

Damn, it just went off two weeks ago. This young bull is always knocking my shit on. That's it, no more for him.

"Don't judge me; he got me fucked up if he thinks he gonna be hitting my shit like this is some young pussy."

I keep the Kitty-kat tight and always make sure it's right.

Chapter 14:
A New Thing

Since I had to leave my young bull alone yet again, I started spending a lot of time with James.

Some Saturdays, I would go over to James's house and chill with him. We would get drunk and then talk about people.

Yo, that's some real fun shit.

As time went on, we started to share some things about ourselves to each other, and I was like: "Wow, I didn't know we had so much in common,"

I saw a side of him that I didn't know existed. That night I learned so much about him that it was such a pull on my spirit.

My feelings grew even stronger for him. And when it came time for us to have sex, it wasn't just having sex for me; I was making love to him.

Everything felt right. He told me to get on my knees and bend over. When I did, he grabbed the oil and then started to rub my ass.

His touch was so gentle, and his voice was soft and comforting.

James: How does that feel?

Stacey: You feel wonderful.

James: Girl, I love your ass and your skin it's so soft.

With a gentle touch, he gripped my hips.

James: Lay down.

I did as he started massaging my hamstrings. Taking his fingertips up and down. He made me feel so relaxed and comfortable.

Then pulling me back to my knees with his hands, he gently stuck the head of his dick inside of me.

Stroking me, teasing me, going in and out. Then he started to have a conversation with me, to see if that was possible, asking me questions.

James: So, how did that massage feel?

Stacey: It, o, it felt soooo good.

James: Girl, your ass is so plump, and your legs are so strong.

Stacey: Ahhhh, that feels so good.

I'm slowly giving it back to him.

James: Tell me, did you work out today?

'Moaning'

Stacey: Ah, Yes.

James: What type of cardio did you do?

Stacey: I did the Ah shit.

Before I was able to finish answering his question, he went in deeper.

James: Are you gonna answer my question?

Stacey: I, I did. Ahhhh. I did the tread, the tread, ah mill.

James: You like the way that feels?

Stacey: Yes

Then, the questions stopped. His fingertips were going up and down my back, scratching it while he stroked my wet kitty.

James: Did you cum yet.

Stacey: Yesss, you feel so good.

He couldn't feel the cum on his dick; I guess because he had on a condom.

James: I want you to cum again.

Then, what surprised me was how he caveman me. He took one hand and threw me over.

James: Lay on your back

I was like: "Pineapples." Damn, did you really have to toss me around like that? To be honest, that kind of turned me on to see that he had some of that up in him.

He then took my legs and spread them apart, and gently put his dick inside of me slowly, going as deep as he can go.

When he hit the point where he couldn't go any further, I screamed his name.

Stacey: JAMES!

I put my hands on his chest as he worked his strokes, using his waist as if he were belly dancing.

Although he was very gentle in his strokes, I still felt as if he were pounding me.

It didn't hurt, but it felt so good as he filled my kitty up with his dick. This nigga was giving me the energy that I needed. Shit! We went at it for about two to three hours.

How could I be so lucky to get this out of men every fucking time? See, this is the kind of shit that spoils a sister and fuck it up for the next guy.

And when he finally got tired, he stopped and says:

James: Okay, that's enough, go to sleep.

Stacey: What!!!

James: You're greedy; you're not getting no more tonight. I'm tired.

Stacey: What!!!!!

Now, we have had discussions about having early morning sex. He said: When I wake up in the morning and that ass is bare and looking at me, I'm gonna stick my dick in it.

So, because he just stopped abruptly, I definitely was expecting him to do what we talked about earlier that day.

When the next morning rolled around, I woke up before he did, and I purposely turned my bare ass around to him, thinking I'm gonna get some more of that long good sex.

And what this nigga does. He got up, turned on the gospel station, and started doing everything else instead of what he said he would do.

I was so fucking mad because of the bullshit he just did. Like, even if he would have come to me for some sex, I wouldn't have been able to give it to him with the gospels on.

You know how it feels when you're expecting something to happen and it doesn't.

A big fucking disappointment.

However, I tried not to show it, so I put my clothes on and left. Fuck it, I'll wash up at home.

And the whole time I were driving home, I just kept telling myself that I wasn't fucking with him no more.

"Don't judge me; I guess I should have been a dude instead."

Chapter 15:
Two Men And A Young Bull

Fuck!!!! I'm still horny. I thought about calling Steph or Rich.

Now as for Rich, I know I wouldn't be able to get in contact with him because he's that type of dude that you won't even hear from unless he's horny for you. He just isn't a basic conversationalist. He always have a motive behind with his words.

And as for Steph, on the other hand, if I say come through, that ass is here and would be down for whatever. Now, I sometimes find myself engaging in conversations with myself. Don't Judge Me; I'm not crazy; I'm just admitting what most people are afraid to admit, not to be looked at differently.

Stacey: Stace, you have to be strong. Don't call Steph one dick at a time. One dick at a time.

But, OMG, I'm so horny.

So, I went into my special drawer and pulled out my vibrator to get rid of that feeling. Normally I can't cum with it.

But, this time, I did and I was so satisfied after that.

Later on, James called me to ask me how did I like his dick and whether or not he satisfied me.

Stacey: You don't need no validation from me. I stayed until the morning, didn't I?

James: Shit, I thought you weren't gonna leave.

Stacey: What!!!!

James: I was a little late doing what I had to do.

Stacey: Oops.

When we hung up, I said: "That's it, I can't with him."

I let two weeks pass with him, telling him my cycle was on. By then, a month has passed and Rich is now texting me.

Rich: Yo shorty.

Stacey: Yo.

Rich: WYD

Stacey: Nothing watching TV.

Rich: I need to see you.

Stacey: No, you mean you want to fuck me.

Rich: No, I want to see you; I miss you.

Stacey: You're not getting no booty.

Rich: That's okay. Can I come over?

Stacey: Come on then.

So, like I said earlier, Rich and I live very close to each other, so he was here in less than ten minutes.

I didn't feel like throwing clothes on, and it's not like he didn't see my bare ass before, anyways.

So, I answered the door with my boxers and a sports bra. The moment that he came in, he gave me a hug with both hands squeezing my ass.

Then we started to kiss. Every time that we kiss it's like lighting a match. Nobody said this better than Michael Jackson, "You wanna be starting something, and you got to be starting something."

Then smelling his cologne on him was like it was grabbing me. It wasn't strong and it wasn't too much, just the right amount.

"Damn, I can't resist this dude." I wanted to take him upstairs and let him fuck me.

But, I have to show some kind of restraint, because:

I don't want a quickie.

Even if he gave me a quickie and say he's gonna take care of me this weekend, it will never happen.

I want the drunk weekend shot because he gets really freaky with it.

That's why.

So we both sat on the couch and just talked, and then he kind of messed me up with the type of questions that he was asking.

For the life of me, I couldn't tell whether he was asking for himself or for someone else. Because he did imply that he was tired and he just wants to chill.

Like I didn't know how to take this part of the conversation because our relationship was like, you come over, or, I come to you, we do what we do, and that's it.

However, I knew that it wasn't gonna get him some booty because one thing for sure and two things for certain: these men will tell you any and everything just to hit one more time.

And what makes matters worse is that this young bull thinks that he could tell me anything. Not knowing, or shall I say, not understanding that I've been around the block a couple of times.

So, I'm not a dumb ass chick to kick game to, like, "Nigga, I don't have a dude for a reason."

When it comes down to something serious, I'm not from Pennsylvania. However, that's where I live,

I'm from the Show Me state, that's where my heart resides. Therefore, anything and everything that you're saying to me, I don't really care.

If you're pulling out your heart, it doesn't mean anything to me unless you're showing me something different.

So, you asking me, what type of man am I interested in? Or the height I prefer my men to be and the age limit in which he has to be.

Then, to already have yourself excluded from the answers to the questions that you ask me was kind of crazy.

All I kept thinking was, dude like I really would consider making your young ass my man.

If you weren't such a bullshitter, that could have been possible.

Like you have to fit somewhere in that equation because we have been messing around with each other for over six months now.

And honestly, if he wanted to be my man, I would have given him that spot. Because sexually, he has it going on.

Anyway, we're still talking, and then he started saying that I could pass for a young girl. About late 30's early 40's.

I'm like: "Shit, I already know that." Then he started touching my legs and talking about how strong they looked.

Rich: Your gym workout is really working for you.

Stacey: Yes. I try not to miss a day I'm on a mission.

Then my phone started ringing back-to-back, and like always when I'm entertaining, I will ignore it.

Rich leaned over and started kissing me passionately and rubbing my breasts. Although I was getting lost in his touch. All I kept telling myself was, "Be strong."

Then he raised my shirt and started nibbling on my nipples. I started moaning because he really knows how I like my breasts handled.

"Damn, he's breaking me."

Stacey: Stop!

Rich: Come on, you know you want it.

Stacey: I do, but I have to get up early for work tomorrow.

Rich: I'll be quick.

Stacey: You know I don't like quickies.

Then he sits up and shows me how hard he is.

Rich: Look what you did to me.

Then he bares himself and tells me to suck it.

Stacey: Nope, it's time for me to go to bed now.

Rich: Come on, just a little.

Stacey: No, you said you just wanted to see me.

Rich: I did.

Stacey: Okay, so you saw me, we talked, and now it's time for you to go.

Well, after I said that to him, his whole facial expression changed; he was mad as hell. I couldn't believe this young bull.

I really emphasize when I say young bull because when he left, he let my stream door slam, and he was literally stomping down the steps.

And when I called his name, he didn't respond. This dude was really throwing a tantrum.

So, I just laughed, closed my door, and took my ass upstairs. When I checked my phone, one of the calls was from James, and the other three were from Steph.

So, which one did I call back? Steph, because I thought it was an emergency. Even though it wasn't and I knew deep down inside of my heart it wasn't.

I just had to call him back first. Because I still love him, even after everything. But he's just not the one for me.

You know, what really makes me mad about him is that now that we're not together, he's always asking if can he take me away somewhere, and I always tell him no, because he never paid for my travel expenses whenever we would go on vacation.

So, why start now? Just to pick up where you left off if I let you back in. HELL NO! You see what I'm saying? Anything to get the kitty-kat.

Shit, he's lucky that I went for that for so long.

You know James is full of surprises; he's calling me again, and this late, OMG. I have to answer this.

James: Hey, what you doing? I've been calling you.

Stacey: You only called me once.

James: I'm gonna leave from your house tomorrow to go to work.

Stacey: Really, are you asking me or telling me?

James: What you have to drink?

Stacey: Moscato and Gin.

James: Alright, cool, have me a glass ready.

Stacey: What?

James: Have my glass ready. I'm looking for parking now.

Stacey: Shit, how long have you been looking for parking?

James: For a minute now.

Stacey: Don't be popping up at my house. What if I had company?

James: Then, that nigga would have to go or get fucked up.

Stacey: You're Funny.

I thought, "Fuck! I hope he didn't see young bull leaving my house."

When we got to the front door, I was already there waiting for him to come in with his drink in my hand.

Stacey: Here.

James: Can I have a kiss?

I gave him a kiss, a little peck on the lips. Then gave him the drink. He took his shoes off, and we went into the dining room.

I tell you, sometimes he scares me. I want to believe that he's all man, but the shit that comes out of his mouth is crazy.

Now, normally, when I buy my bananas, they're medium with brown spots or medium and half green and yellow.

They're never completely ripe. Except this time, they were very much yellow, long, and kind of thick.

So, when he saw the bananas on the table, he asked can he get one. Now, here's the thing: the way that he asked was like:

James: Can I get one of those big yellow dicks.

Hold the fuck up, my lips were poked out, and my eyebrows furrowed.

Stacey: WHAT!!!!

His hand was moving in a kind of way that a woman would move hers. So, I had to ask:

Stacey: Why would you refer to the banana as that?

James: Because that's what it looks like.

Stacey: Not to me.

At that time, I wondered if he went both ways. He's brown skin with a brown dick. And his dick do not look nothing like a fucking banana.

Not to mention that he likes light skin females with big butts. So, he probably likes light-skinned dudes.

Oh my God. Please, God, I hope he's not that way. "An undercover brother going both ways."

Then his voice got a little sweet. Maybe it's my brain now taking me places because I now have this thought in my head.

James: Girl, you know it does, stop playing. I'm surprised you don't have it up in you.

Stacey: WHAT!!!!! Why would I when I could get the real light skin dick?

James: Stop talking shit and make me another drink.

Stacey: The bottles are right there; make your own.

James: Damn, girl, do I need to check your temperature?

Stacey: My temp is good. Shit! Do I need to check your temperature?

James: What's on under that robe?

Stacey: You're about to see in a minute. Turn off the lights, let's go.

He turned the lights off and followed me upstairs with the drink in his hand.

However, we didn't get the chance to make it all the way up because, he lifted up my robe and saw that I had nothing on underneath it.

James: Oh shit, look at all that big red ass.

He was so excited when he saw my bare ass that he told me to bend over and spread my legs apart as much as I could on the steps.

I did. I got on my knees and spread my legs, and stuck my big fat ass out. And there he surprised me again.

He opened my cheeks and started licking me from my ass to my kitty.

Once he reached my kitty-kat, he stuck his tongue so deep inside of me.

Wow, his tongue is so long and thick, it felt like a dick going inside of me.

Stacey: OOOooo

James: You like this?

Stacey: Yes.

Then he stuck his thumb in my ass, and his trigger finger started massaging my kitty as he nibbled on my ass cheeks.

Stacey: Damn!

James: You want it?

Stacey: Yes.

James: Come on, let's go upstairs.

As I was turning back around to go upstairs James picked up his drink and took a big gulp.

James: Damn, that was good.

I took two steps up when he grabbed my ass.

James: Stop, fuck it. I want you right here. That ass is saying take me.

I got back on my knees, and he rammed his dick inside of me, and I screamed.

Stacey: Awwww.

As he was fucking me hard. And with every scream:

James: This is what you wanted.

Stacey: Yes.

James: You like it like this, don't you?

Stacey: Yes

I felt his dick growing inside of me even more.

Stacey: It's too much. James, James, it's too much.

James: No, it's not. Take it.

Stacey: I can't.

I don't know what got into him that night. Maybe, his dude didn't suck him off really good because he was no longer that gentle lover, or maybe he was showing me that he could fuck hard and that he is all man.

I don't know, but that night, he had Steph and Rich up in him. "Damn, how can I let him go now. Fuck."

Stacey: OMG, I'm coming again.

James: Give it to me.

Stacey: Take it, take it.

He began ramming himself harder inside of me. I grab the pole of the banister, holding it tight so that my face won't be pushed into the step.

My body was jerking with every pound; it felt as if he were hitting my lower abdomen.

Then he pulled back and just gave me the head, hitting my G-spot. My feet began to curl as I started to have an orgasm.

Stacey: Awwwwww Shit.

He started fucking me fast as he went deep again. I could hear the wetness from my kitty as it flowed out like a faucet being turned on.

His testicles were so fucking wet as they slapped against my inner thigh that all you could hear was the slapping noise.

Damn, I came so fucking much that it drained the fuck out of me. Then he stopped.

James: Come on I want to finish with you on the bed.

So, he grabbed my waist and pulled me up to my feet, then turned me around and picked me up, then threw me over his shoulders.

As he walked through the hallway to the room, I can see him waddling like a penguin because his pants were hanging from his hips.

Then he took me in the room and tossed me on the bed. I just wanted to stay there in the position that he put me in and go to sleep.

James: Come on, girl, you act like you don't get enough; now I'm here, and I'm gonna fuck you all night until you can't take it no more.

Stacey: I can't take no more. No, I want to go to sleep.

James: Not tonight.

Stacey: Please we could finish in the morning.

James: Nope.

He opened my legs and started sucking and biting on my thighs.

Stacey: Ah, ah, ah, that hurts, you're biting too hard.

Then he took his fingers and gently scratched down my inner thighs, and his mouth went from one side to the other as he nibbled on them.

I said to myself, "Damn, he never did this before."

James: Yeah, girl, you think I'm gonna let you get away this time? You and that good ass pussy belong to me.

In my head, I was like: "What! This is not yours. We're just linking up.

James: Stacey, where's the vibrator?

Stacey: Under the pillow.

He got the vibrator from under the pillow, turned it on then put it on my kitty-kat. Then he took his one finger and stuck it inside of me, wiggling my G-spot as he sucked on my breast.

"Damn, his sex game went to ten; I'm impressed." Then my notifications started going off. I was getting all these damn text messages.

Then the doorbell started ringing over and over as if there was some type of emergency.

James: You want me to stop so you can get the door?

Stacey: No, no, please don't, they'll go away.

Then there was a hard banging knock on the door, like the way the Police would bang on it.

I couldn't zone that out. It actually could be the Police.

Stacey: Damn, baby, stop. Let me see who it is.

I got up, grabbed my robe from out the inside closet door, and went downstairs to answer the door.

"Man, this shit better be important, or somebody's getting cursed out."

When I opened the door, it was that damn Steph.

Steph: Stacey, can I talk to you for a minute?

Stacey: About what, what's so damn important that you had to come over here unannounced.

Steph: Baby, I miss the hell out of you, and I'm sorry. I'm a changed man; if you give me the opportunity to show you, you will not regret it. I promise.

Stacey: Look, I don't have time for this tonight.

Steph: Can I come in?

Stacey: No, I'm busy.

Steph: What? You have a nigga in there?

Stacey: Boy, bye.

When I went to close the door, Steph stuck his foot in between the doorway.

Stacey: Would you move your foot?

Steph: Stacey, who the fuck you have in there?

Stacey: None of your business, nigga! My house.

This shit turned out to be a whole argument. Then, to add to it, James comes downstairs with his gun in his hand, ready as he confronts Steph.

James: Nigga, is there a problem? I heard my lady tell you to leave.

I was stunned because when did I become his lady? I guess that's why he was giving me level 10.

Shaking my head right now.

Steph didn't really have anything to say back to James; his toughness was no longer there.

The energy that Steph gave to me, he didn't dare to give to James. The look on Steph's face was like, this is a big nigga. Like, don't even say anything; just walk away.

And surprisingly, that's exactly what he did. He turned around and walked his ass back down the steps.

James: And nigga don't call her anymore, or I'm gonna have to come to where you live.

Stacey: Yo, what are you doing? You didn't have to do all that.

James: What! You taking up for that disrespectful weak ass nigga? Trying to barge his way in against your will, oh, you still want him.

Stacey: What! I'm gonna need you to chill the fuck out because you're doing too much. You know what, yall motherfuckers done messed up my vibe. It's time for you to go.

James: Not until I'm finished.

Stacey: You are finished.

James got down on his knees and crawled up to me. For a second, I thought that he was about to propose.

I'm not gonna lie; I got a little excited because I was like, "Finally. I'm gonna get me a husband."

But he fooled the shit out of me. He crawled up to me, opened my robe, and started licking my kitty-kat.

I mean, he literally had my shit in his mouth while his tongue went to work. "Damn nigga, let me close the door."

After a while, it was like, fuck the door being cracked because he was feeling good as hell.

Stacey: Oh my goodness, I'm cumming.

I leaned back on the door; it slammed shut. I grabbed his head with one hand and covering my mouth with the other because I didn't want the people that were outside to hear.

James: I told you this is my pussy, and I'll pop a motherfucker for it too.

Right then and there, he had me kind of scared because he's changed.

I don't think I want this, James. So quick to pull out his gun and pop someone.

James: I'm gonna sign my name all over that pussy.

Stacey: What!!

James: Bend over across the chair.

Stacey: Nigga hell no, I already have to clean my steps.

So, he got up off the floor and grabbed my hand, pulling me to the steps.

James: Right here, put one leg on the third step like you're skipping steps.

I did, and he started eating it again. I couldn't take it anymore; my kitty felt like I had a vibrator on it all day. So sensitive.

When I told him I was done, he bent me over on the steps and started fucking me like he was mad at me.

It was no longer feeling good. That shit was very painful; it felt like he was trying to open a new hole.

All I kept thinking was, why do these motherfuckers keep fucking me like that.

If I didn't know any better, I would think that he was fucking me with attitude.

He had me screaming with every pump; I started pleading with him to stop. Like, what's up with these motherfuckers, with the angry fucks?

Stacey: Stop, please stop; I can't take it; it's hurting. Ahhh.

James: I told you I'm signing my name in this pussy, it belongs to me now.

Stacey: Please stop.

I started crying, then he came out of me and started rubbing all over my ass, gently sucking my ass cheeks.

Then he took his fingernails and started to scratch down the center of my back, relaxing me.

James: I'm sorry, baby.

He kissed down the center of my back to my ass.

James: I didn't mean to hurt you; I lost myself in you for a moment; please forgive me. I love you; I don't want to hurt you.

I didn't say anything because I was mad as hell at him for beating up my kitty like that. He knows I can't take his big ass dick.

It felt like he was taking his anger out on me from Steph popping up at my front door.

After he got finished rubbing and kissing on me to put me in a comfortable state of mind once more, I had a déjà vu. Everything that he said and did was like he read the same damn handbook.

James: Baby, can I get some more, so I can cum? I promise I won't hurt you. As a matter of fact, let's go upstairs to the room.

We went to the room, and I just laid down in the bed, and he laid on the other side of me, then he tapped my arm.

I was so tired and exhausted.

Stacey: What!

James: Baby, turn on your side.

I turned on my side with my ass facing him, and he stuck himself in me slowly; with every stroke, it matched mines; we were on one accord, totally in sync with each other.

Now, it was feeling amazing. Occasionally, he went deep with the head of his dick, reaching the top of my kitty very gently.

For that moment he brought back that gentle lover that I used to know. I was in total ecstasy; he had me calling out his name.

Stacey: Yes, James, Oh yes, yes baby, yes, oh, that feels so good.

His stroke got a little harder, but not to the point that it was hurting. For I knew he was about to cum.

He grabbed my shoulder, pushing my body down on him, and I grabbed his ass with my one hand pushing him into me, for I was about to have another orgasm.

His hard, slow pumps became harder and faster, and his grip tighter. Shit, don't think for a second that I wasn't throwing that shit back on him because the both of us started to have an orgasm at the same time.

Stacey: Ah, ah, yes, I'm cumming

James: Ummmmmm, shittttttt.

That was awesome; we both came at the same time. Cool, because, now I could go to sleep.

You know, sometimes after sex, I just want to cuddle, but James is not that person. However, Steph is, and I miss that about him.

"Damn, I wonder how long did that session last? It feels like it was on all night."

Thirty minutes later, James jumps up and starts to get dressed dramatically.

Stacey: Where you going?

James: Oh my bad, I have to leave because I'm going through something right now.

Stacey: What!!!!

James: I'll tell you later.

Stacey: You know what, get your shit on and go then, hurry up so I can go to sleep

James: Come on, baby, you don't have to be like that.

Stacey: Yes, I do, you doing that? Oh nigga, it's like that.

As this nigga was getting dressed, I had all sorts of thoughts going through my mind.

He has to hurry home to someone.

He has to meet up with someone, a female, of course.

It has to be another female involved.

So, all that shit he just did, for what? Oh, this nigga likes to have all icing on the cake.

"Motherfucker." I can't, I'm done.

After that, he didn't text nor call nor did I. We didn't speak to one another for about two months.

Although I knew neither one of these dick heads wasn't good for me, I still found myself back in their clutches.

One Saturday night, Rich called, and I wasn't doing nothing but trying on clothes that I bought online and getting my drink on. He asked:

Rich: Hey beautiful, what are you doing, can I come to see you?

Stacey: Sure.

Shit, it wasn't like I had plans for that night, and besides, I didn't have any sex in a while, and at this point, I'm feeling my drinks, and I could really go for a nice piece of that light-skin love.

"Don't judge me. Like I said earlier, all that young bull has to really do is call."

When he came over, I was lying on the chair with my drink in my hand. He asked if he could have something to drink, too.

I told him to go get it himself. Listen, when you come over to my house the first couple of times, you're my guest; you will get the best hospitality from me four to five times.

By the sixth time, it's, nigga help yourself because motherfucker's be thinking that they have a maid.

"Don't judge me; the company will have me like that because they take advantage of that shit."

But, on some real shit, I was just too damn drunk to be waiting on someone. After he made his drink, I told him to go upstairs and get naked and wait for me. I'm gonna finish my drink, then I'll be there.

He kind of looked confused, like: "Hun." So I repeated myself, and he darted up the steps.

Chapter 16:
Temperature Rising

By the time I came upstairs, Rich had his clothes on the floor as if his ass were home, laying in the middle of the bed with his arms and legs stretched out.

Now for him to be a young bull, he did some old head shit. In the bed with his damn socks on. Long white socks, at that.

"What the fuck."

Stacey: Boy, if you don't take off those damn socks!

He took them off, and then I got my oil and started to give him a full body massage. But, hold on, let me set the mood because it was dark as shit in my bedroom.

So, I lit a scented candle. Then, I told Alexa to play my slow jams. As she started off playing Rihanna's "Skin," I started to dance as I was stripping.

Taking everything off except the pink lace panties. Then I climbed over him and started to massage his foot.

Now let me tell you about the bull's foot. They were hard as hell. It felt like he had calluses on them.

No wonder he got in the bed with those damn socks on. I would have, too.

To show him that I can enjoy his whole body, I still sucked on his toes. One by one, I rubbed up and down his feet.

I wonder what was he thinking while I was doing that. Shit! He probably was saying, "Damn, she's drunk as shit."

After I was done with his toes, I crawled up on the bed, imagining myself as a cheetah, whose about to eat her prey.

I took my tongue and licked up the top of his feet as I slowly rubbed up his legs, then gently scratched down.

His ass was like:

Rich: Ahhh.

Once I heard that, it put fuel into my body. Then I went up to his thighs and started rubbing him and gently biting on him.

He was so turned on that his dick was sticking straight up in the air.

So I crawled some more, and with my lips, I grabbed one of his balls, putting it in my mouth.

Rich: Oh shit!!!

I'm sucking it, pulling it gently. Then I worked my way back down his legs, crawling like the cheetah I imagined myself to be as I nibbled gently.

Occasionally, I pulled on his skin with my teeth in between his thighs as I rubbed the front of his legs.

Rich: Aw shit.

Then, I repeated the process over with the other side, but this time, when I got up to his balls, I licked in between the two and all the way to the head of his dick.

He was going crazy. That shit pushed another button.

"Don't judge me; he gets me this way."

So, I put his dick completely in my mouth and took as much as I could until I started choking.

Rich: Oh shit, girl! What the fuck are you doing to me?

He grabbed my head, and before he got the chance to push me down on him. I slapped the shit out of his hands.

Stacey: Don't fucking touch me. Just lay there. Now say you're sorry.

Rich: Oh shit! I'm sorry. Please forgive me. Please don't stop.

Then I gently started nibbling around his dick and in between his thighs, working my way up and down, teasing the shit out of him.

His fucking dick didn't have any more room, he was super hard. I thought his dick was about to split at any moment.

So now I'm working my way up his chest. I grabbed my vibrator from under the pillow, turned it on, and put it on his balls as I sucked and nibbled on him.

Rich: Ahhhhhh, oh shit, ah

I knew I had him, I'm about to turn this young bull completely out.

Rich: Please, Stace, please. Can I taste it?

I started to lick him as I crawled up to his neck, working my tongue around to his ear, putting it in my mouth, and sucking on it while having the vibrator now on the head of his dick.

Rich: Oh yes, please let me taste it.

I climbed up on him and sat on his dick. I screamed for he felt like a wooden stick.

Stacey: Ahhhhhh, fuck, you're so fucking hard it hurts.

We started kissing so passionately, and then he grabbed me, and I got up.

Stacey: I told you not to fucking touch me. Now, turn around.

Rich: Damn Stace! I'm sorry, you feel so fucking wet.

Stacey: I don't want to hear that shit. Turn the fuck around.

He turned around and laid on his stomach. I started massaging his neck as I licked down his bald head.

I worked my way down his back, nibbling on his neck as my hands kept working their way down to his ass.

I licked down his spine then I started to massage his ass and biting on his cheeks.

Rich: Oh shit!

He was moving all around. For a second, I thought that he was expecting me to lick his asshole.

This young bull is some kind of freaky, but I'm not even putting my tongue in his ass. Wrong chick. The ass says exit, not enter.

Then I got up, I told him to turn back around, and when he did, I climbed up on him backward, putting all this ass in his face as I sat on his dick again, slowly going down on it, taking it as far as it would go.

Stacey: Ahhhh shit, it hurts Rich.

I bent over and grabbed the calf of his legs as I started to ride him.

Rich: Oh my God, I'm ready to cum.

Stacey: No.

I got up.

Rich: Please let me lick it. Please!

I turned around and climbed up to his face, squatting over him, putting the very tip of his tongue on my clitoris.

He then began to move his tongue up and down as I stayed there in position, holding on to the high backboard of the bed.

Then he wrapped his arms around my legs, pushing me up further, and started licking my ass.

Now, for me, that felt just a little weird, it always has. There was a part of me that wanted to say: "Pineapples" because my mind keeps telling me exit only.

It's just weird.

"Don't judge me; the back door is for exiting, not entering."

So, I moved my ass backward, putting his tongue back on my clitoris, and once again, he put me back into that mood.

He had me feeling so good. All I kept saying to myself was, "This fucking young ass boy is turning me out. Shit, he could always get this."

I started going up and down, moving all around his mouth.

Stacey: Ahhhh, Ahhhh, Rich, Ahhhh, it feels so fucking good. Ah, you gonna make me cum.

Rich: Come on, I want you to cum in my mouth.

After that, I got on top and started riding him as if I were riding a stallion, going crazy on the dick.

He had me just that excited. Even though it was hurting, it also felt good. I felt him in my stomach.

His dick was hitting every wall. He had me screaming and hitting him on his chest to stop.

Then he put his hand around my throat and applied pressure. I didn't know how to take that one.

It did take away the pain from him beating up the kitty because it had me up in my head thinking some other shit.

Like, is he trying to kill me or something? But it didn't have me gasping for air, so I guess this was the new thing now.

To be honest, I'm still trying to figure out whether I like that or not. You know, not all sex is good sex.

The one thing that I could say about Young Bull is that he introduced me to something different after dealing with men my age.

And he would be the one that I would keep around to satisfy my sexual needs.

Rich: Turn around, get on your knees, I want to smack that big red ass.

I turned around.

Rich: Now, come to the edge of the bed

I came to the edge of the bed. And he rammed his dick in me hard. I screamed.

Stacey: Ah, it hurts, it hurts

I tried to move up and away from him. But he grabbed my thighs and pulled me back into him.

Rich: Where you going? Get back here. There's no running today. You feel this?

Stacey: Ye, Ye, it hurts so bad. Ahhhhh

Rich: You could take it. You got it like this.

Stacey: No, I can't. It hurts; you're too much.

Rich: I'm about to cum.

Man, that was like music to my ears because he was really beating the shit out of my kitty.

"Don't judge me; I thought I could handle him this time."

He grabbed me tighter, digging his fingers into my legs, pumping faster and harder.

I put my face into the pillow because I was screaming as if he were stabbing me in my kitty-kat. Then he started getting loud.

Rich: Oh Shit, Oh Shit, I'm fucking cumming.

Stacey: Ahhhhh

We both came at the same time. After our orgasm, he backed up; I could tell that he was completely drained or he was just as drunk as I was because he almost fell backward.

After catching himself, he then put his hands on the sides of his head then stood there.

Rich: Damn girl, I came a lot, you have some good pussy.

Stacey: You see what happens when you make me wait.

After a couple of minutes of him standing there, he went to take the condom off, and the look he had on his face was like, "Fuck."

Stacey: What's wrong, why you're looking at me like that?

Rich: The condom busted.

Stacey: What!!!!!

I didn't want to hear that shit. Like, "hell to the fucking no." Do I want another baby? Nah, and I know that his soldiers are marching strong.

And looking at him he was still hard. I was like, "Oh shit, let's have it." Right now, I want some more.

Whatever happens, happens. I'll deal with it later.

"Don't judge me; I'm just greedy like that."

I got out the bed and went to him and gave him one of my most passionate kisses as I rubbed his head.

And once again, he was ready. The scare of the condom breaking went out the door.

Rich: Lay down

I laid down, but before he stuck his dick in me.

Rich: I only brought one condom with me. Can I go raw? I want to feel you.

And honestly, at that point, I didn't care because he just got finished ejaculating all in me, so if anything was to transpire, it would already be in the making.

I just couldn't get enough of him. That night, I must have had about ten orgasms to his two. I was completely drained of all fluids and energy.

My kitty-kat was so sore that when he came out, it still felt like he was in there.

Chapter 17: The Test

OMG, I really got some good ass sleep that night. Now, normally, after we're done, he would just get up, put his clothes on, and go home.

But not this time. He fell back on the pillow, and before I knew it, I thought there was a truck in my bed. That's how hard he slept.

I just laughed and let him stay there for a moment. Since he was there, I thought that I would just lay beside him and fall asleep in his arms, but that wasn't happening.

Shit! That nigga definitely needs a C-Pak. It was time for that ass to go now.

"Don't judge me; sleep is everything to me."

So I woke that ass up because I couldn't even cuddle with him, nor could I lay beside him and fall asleep, Shit! If I couldn't get no sleep in my own damn bed, then why the fuck should he. So he got up and dressed, then left. But wait the fuck a minute. Let me back this shit up just a little.

This motherfucker gone ask me for some money so he can get something to eat. Talking about he left his wallet at home. "Nigga please, I don't give nigga's money,"

Wrong person. Like, you really live ten minutes away; you can wait until you get home.

Shit, I guess that ass gone be hungry then because we're not gonna start this shit. I don't play those games, and I don't pay for sex.

"Sorry, BooBoo."

Stacey: Nah, I don't have no money on me; my cash stays in the bank, not in my pockets.

This young bull had this look on his face like, "What! She told me no. After I gave her all this dick."

Stacey: Why you looking like that?

Rich: Because I know you have it.

Stacey: I do have it in the bank.

Rich: Every woman keeps money around the house at all times.

Stacey: Sorry, not this one.

Then I thought about it. "Was this a test to see if he could get some money from me?"

Because it would have started at ten dollars, then he'll start going higher. Fuck that, I guess I failed that test.

In my Berney Mac voice, "You ain't gon' get Nothing, Nothing, Nothing." You know, I just couldn't understand why his ass got mad over ten dollars.

His confidence in his sex game is too fucking high for him to bring money into the equation.

Shit! That young motherfucker gonna learn today.

Chapter 18: Choices

Saturday morning, and I'm getting so many text messages waking me the fuck up from a good ass sleep.

You know motherfuckers just didn't understand the night I had.

Stacey: Alexa, what time is it?

Alexa: The time is 6: 00 am.

I'm like, "6 am, what the fuck!"

So when I looked at my phone, I had 10 text messages, six were from Rich, two were from Steph, and two from James.

Rich messages were like:

1. Good morning on my way to work, just thinking about you.
2. Damn girl, you wore me out.
3. You're nasty; I love it.
4. I'm already on my second cup of coffee.
5. We have to hook up again.
6. Girl, girl, girl.

My response was like: Hun, this nigga just trying to get some more of me. Fuck out-of-here. That's not gonna happen.

Now last but not least, this crazy ass James who thinks the sun rises and set on that ass.

James' messages were like:

1. Yo baby, give me a call; our appointment is today. Miss you.
2. Miss you, sorry, call me I want to see you.

My response was like: What fucking appointment. Yo, this nigga always speaking some crazy shit.

I'm not fucking with you no more. Like nigga you just want some ass.

After being with Rich about a month ago, I realized that my cycle didn't come on. Being pregnant never crossed my mind.

I thought that I started to go through the changes (menopause) until six weeks later when I started to feel nauseous and sleepy all the damn time.

I needed to be certain, so I went and brought me a pregnancy test. And guess what? It came back positive.

"God dammit," I didn't know that I could still get pregnant because as much as Steph came inside of me that never happened.

Maybe because his sperm cells weren't strong enough due to the fact that he has medical issues and the meds that he takes lower his chance of even making a baby.

Now, here's the questions that I kept fighting with myself over and over with. But then I knew that wouldn't be a good thing.

1. Am I gonna keep it?
2. And if I do, will I tell him or just sell my house, quit my job, and move down south, because lord knows I wouldn't raise any more kids in Philly.
3. Or do I put it up for adoption and continue with my life?

Decisions, decisions.......

Like it should be a no-brainer, but this dude is always getting me caught up in his web.

At one point I did think about telling him and maybe having him move into my house so that we could co-parent if I decided to keep it.

I mean, that would be good for me because then I could get the dick almost every night. It would be one or the other, me wearing that ass out or me getting warn out. Either way, it would be good for me and my sex drive.

But then I knew that that wouldn't be a good thing. And to be honest, I low-key fell in love with him too and wanted to be with him but he has too much of that young bull mentality going on.

"Don't judge me; this is what the fuck I get. I'm already judging myself."

Now, seven weeks into my pregnancy, I still didn't tell him. The sex was hurting so bad as he pounded on my ass, doggy style.

Sometimes, it was a fight just to get him to stop or slow down. Even though it would hurt like crazy, I would still give it to him because it was satisfying. And, because now, I would have to keep my baby's daddy around.

That one session would last me for about 2 to 3 days before I needed another one. Okay, y'all, as embarrassing as this sounds, I'm gonna give y'all some truth.

I was dick whipped by his young ass. I didn't want it, I needed it. Then I fell in love with it. Not with him.

"Don't judge me, Good dick will make you that way."

He was just a package deal because if I could take him as my loyal subject or, shall I say, servant, he will live under me.

The dick will follow me where ever I go, just in case I get horny.

"Don't judge me. Young bull is big."

So, after telling my girlfriend about the baby, she was very excited. She was ready to be a Godmother.

Shit, did I really want to be a mother at my age and give up my fun and my lifestyle?

Me getting pregnant was not a part of the plan, but that young bull and his cheap ass condoms trying to set me the fuck up. Shaking my head!

I had some shit to think about. Like, no, the fuck I don't, this baby has to go.

So, I made my appointment with the doctor to handle that. A week has passed, and now I'm 8 weeks. By the time I went to see the doctor, the baby had died.

I think it was because of the pills I was taking for my bladder infection. Oh well, back to doing me. This time, I gotta be more careful; there can't be any more mistakes.

So now that my body is healing, I really don't want to see anyone right now. I'd rather just take the time out for me.

Because nobody's getting any of the kitty-kat, and as for that light skin motherfucker, his ass is on punishment for trying to get me caught up.

Like, how dare he? You know what, it's time for me to meet some fresh meat. I guess I'll go back to the online dating site. I might just find my husband in the other race. Wouldn't that be some shit?

"Don't judge me, just a little tired of black men."

Chapter 19:
Mind, Body And Soul

Another week passed and now I'm back in the gym. Working on body, mind, and soul.

You know, when you're determined and passionate about something, you tend to put your all into it.

Well, that's what I do. So today, in the gym, I worked the living shit out of myself. 3-mile run on the treadmill and a power walk for 1 mile at 4.0 on a 7.5 incline.

My fucking thighs were feeling it. Then, I did 100 crunches, 100 side bends, 100 bends, and 100 back kicks.

Oh shit, I can't leave out 20 minutes on the stair master and 60 chest presses.

Because the legs have to stay looking tight, the breast must stay perky, and the booty definitely have to stay lifted and right.

I'm back at it bitches, don't hate the player; hate the motherfucken game. So watch your boyfriends and your husbands because, with this hourglass figure, he's definitely gonna be looking hard and wishing or trying to holla.

Don't be mad at me; it's not a me problem; it's a you problem. Check him. If his coins is long and, he can take care of me like he is doing you.

Then, "Don't judge me if I decide to holla back. Because that love shit is out the door."